SHE WASN'T GORGE~~...~~
HER EFFECT WAS LETHAL . . .

Sheila O'Connor led the handsome, tuxedoed stranger to her car. It was a Jaguar XJ6, parked on Amsterdam Avenue, just behind the Metropolitan Opera House. As Sheila led him to it, she hummed, both to quell her mounting agitation as well as to prevent conversation between them.

"What are you humming?" he asked.

She smiled mysteriously and shrugged.

As they got to the sedan, she withdrew the car keys from her purse and, crossing to the driver's door, handed them to him. He unlocked the door.

Sheila retrieved the keys, slid into the driver's seat, turned on the ignition and, smiling, patted the seat next to her.

He crossed in front of the car to occupy it.

She floored the accelerator and the car lurched forward, knocking him up on the hood. She reversed, then floored it again and felt the car bounce as it passed over him; first the front wheels, then the back. She reversed the process and felt the double bounce again before she drove quickly away.

Finding herself humming the same tune again, she laughed aloud. If you follow Amsterdam Avenue south, it turns into Tenth Avenue, and that was the melody and the reason for it. *Slaughter on Tenth Avenue* . . .

BOB RANDALL

THE LAST MAN ON THE LIST

POCKET BOOKS

New York   London   Toronto   Sydney   Tokyo   Singapore

An *Original* Publication of POCKET BOOKS

POCKET BOOKS, a division of Simon & Schuster Inc.
1230 Avenue of the Americas, New York, NY 10020

ISBN: 0-671-68651-8

First Pocket Books printing December 1990

10 9 8 7 6 5 4 3 2 1

POCKET and colophon are registered trademarks of
Simon & Schuster Inc.

Printed in the U.S.A.

FOR JULIA, EDWARD, AND GARY.
IN ORDER OF APPEARANCE.

1

Sheila wasn't gorgeous, though you'd think she was if you passed her at a gallery opening or a benefit for the ballet scholarship fund; but the truth was that she wasn't gorgeous. Her *effect,* however, was lethal.

She stared at the flaws in her face (such as they were), which were exaggerated by the magnifying makeup mirror in her bathroom. She was small-eyed like her mother's mother, the one'd who made them wipe their feet before they entered her apartment to receive her perfunctory kisses and her scrupulous examinations for dirt. Her nose was, of course, perfect, for perfect noses money can buy. Her mouth was sensuous and turned down at the ends; her lips, painted in three shades of rose to emphasize their fullness, stretched over two symmetrical rows of braced-capped-bonded teeth, which, like her nose, were perfect and expensive.

Her hair had been kinky and drab once upon a time, but since her eighteenth birthday—when Sheila O'Connor, as she was then, had reinvented herself—it had hung straight and auburn to the nape of her neck.

She stepped out of the bathroom into her dressing

room and stood before its full-length mirror. Blass's little black dress was an appropriate choice, as were the Kenneth Cole pumps. She wore no scent this evening, and that gave her the odd sensation of being in disguise.

"You still here?" Her husband, whose ample behind sat on several companies' boards, leaned into the room.

"Yes."

She held up her hands and scrutinized her nails, which radiated out like ten perfect, bleeding little soldiers.

"Is there something going on after the opera?" Harold asked.

"Like what?"

"I don't know. A benefit. For homeless supernumeraries or third-world cymbalists . . ."

"There's nothing going on. I'll be home around eleven." She hoped that would end the conversation.

"Okay, toots," and he left the room, but not before Sheila winced at the appellation.

Later, in the elevator going down to the lobby, a woman in mink seethed over Sheila's red fox. Jackie Gleason was right. How sweet it is.

Qual che nume ciha fatti capitar . . . capitar . . . capitar . . . capitar.
Sheila hardly noticed the second act of *The Marriage of Figaro* come to a close, so intent was her concentration on the man in the row ahead of her. His hair was silver (where Harold's was gray), his tuxedo by Perry Ellis and not, mercifully, Brooks

Brothers; his nails were manicured and he wore no wedding band, though she was sure he was married.

The object of her constant gaze now stood up and sidestepped to the aisle. She waited until he had passed her row and then, stepping over those who made no attempt to make her passage easier, fought her way to the aisle and followed him.

He sauntered with his hands in his pants pockets, which lifted his jacket in back, permitting Sheila to admire his small, high ass. Her brother had had such an ass until years of sitting behind computers on Long Island had spread it to its current state. She thought briefly of her brother, Sean, and his wife and their three waistless children, and smiled at her life compared to theirs.

He reached the back of the auditorium, and they were suddenly separated by half a dozen cigarette-starved typists who, it seemed from their chatter, were here on the proceeds of their weekly poker game. Sheila pushed her way around them in time to see him start up the stairs to the family circle.

She caught his profile; not bad, not bad at all. At least his chin was singular, unlike a certain husband whose attitude toward liposuction was as antique as it was infuriating.

And then she remembered that it didn't matter anymore.

He entered the opera bar, and she after him. As he ordered a drink, Sheila caught sight of herself reflected in a silver water pitcher. She looked stunning and, like it or not, the time had come to act. She came up beside him.

It took eight minutes for them to decide to skip the rest of the opera.

A couple of art students who were sitting beside the fountain in the Lincoln Center plaza (for lack of money to do anything else) watched Sheila and the man stride past. The girl fantasized about being the woman on the arm of a powerful man. The boy merely wondered what kind of car they drove.

It was a Jaguar XJ6, parked on Amsterdam Avenue behind the opera house. As Sheila led him to it, she hummed, both to quell her mounting agitation and to prevent conversation between them.

"What are you humming?" he asked.

She smiled mysteriously and shrugged.

As they reached the sedan, she withdrew the car keys from her purse and, crossing to the driver's door, handed them to him. He took them without surprise. Sheila was right. He was not the kind who enjoyed standing by idly while women opened doors of any kind for themselves.

He unlocked the door and slowly pulled it open as wide as it would go, turning a mechanical maneuver into a sexual gesture.

Sheila retrieved the keys, slid into the driver's seat, turned on the ignition, and, smiling, patted the seat next to her.

He crossed in front of the car to occupy it.

She floored the accelerator and the car lurched forward, knocking him up onto the hood. She put it in reverse and floored it again. He slid off the polished metal and fell into the gutter in front of the car.

She drove forward and felt the car bounce as it passed over him: first the front wheels, then the back. She reversed the process and then, putting it in drive, felt the double bounce again before she pulled out onto the avenue and quickly drove north.

On the way to the garage, she complimented herself on choosing Harold's five-thousand-pound Jaguar for the evening, rather than her own lightweight Mercedes coupe. And finding herself humming the same tune again, she recognized it and laughed aloud.

If you follow Amsterdam Avenue south, it turns into Tenth Avenue, and that was the melody and the reason for it. "Slaughter on Tenth Avenue."

2

Hal Fisher sank down into the couch of the writers' room of Studio 104.

"If Glenda fucks up the next line," he said, staring at the pretty woman on the TV monitor in front of him, "I vote we disembowel her."

The actress did indeed fuck up the next line by inverting two key words, and still the studio audience laughed long and hard.

"They love her, the morons," Hal said, flicking a carob-covered almond at her image so that it ricocheted off the screen and landed somewhere under a bank of equipment.

"Oh, my God, we'll get roaches," Betty Lancing whined. Betty was new to New York and to roaches. Several months before, she and her partner, Andy Moffatt, had been writing a children's show in L.A. When Betty heard that Hal Fisher, the creator of *Family Business* was coming to town, she had besieged Andy until he agreed to their writing a sample script. And now here they were.

"Roaches are our friends," Hal said. "It's actors who are our enemies."

"I like Glenda. She's funny," Andy said, and Hal pelted him with an almond.

"Children, listen to me." Hal summoned up his most rabbinical, wisdom-laden voice. "We are writers. We are mongeese. Actors are cobras. If you turn your back on an actor, he will bite your ass and have his agent demand five more points for the privilege."

"Mongooses," Betty said.

"I'm talking ultimate truth and she's correcting my English." Hal flicked an almond at her.

"Stop it! Nobody cleans this place," and Betty pulled her feet up under her as if there were already roaches dashing into the room who had heard about the flying feast.

Whereupon Glenda skipped three lines entirely and said the fourth one in reverse.

Stu Harris, the sitcom's director, was sitting in the control room in front of a bank of monitors, calling camera shots, as Hal came in and made his way through a sea of associate producers, coordinating producers, assistant producers, executive producers, and just plain producers to his friend's ear.

"Our fucking star is doing somebody else's show tonight. Do you think you could remind her that this is *Family Business* and not *Family Ties* before I lose my temper and give her a hysterectomy?"

"She said something wrong?"

Hal winced. "Not if you think 'Take my wife, please' and 'Would you please take my wife' are the same thing."

"I can't reshoot. I got a ten o'clock with my shrink."

"Stuart," Hal whispered, "may your next marriage take place in California and may community property once again leave you with one ball." He turned to the throng between him and the door. "And God parted the producers and Moses left Egypt." They made a path, and Hal returned to his staff and his almonds.

The plot of the episode (unlike its dialogue) intact, the weekly solution to the weekly problem attained, the taping ended. The audience, as usual, resisted leaving the studio, hoping to get a closer look at Glenda Carpenter, who was already eating a bag of White Castle hamburgers in her limo on the way to Connecticut and her dogs.

Hal busily looked for someone with whom to play. Betty had a date with an Aryan copywriter for dinner and indiscriminate but safe sex. Andy had a similar engagement with a similar young man. Stu was in a cab heading up the West Side, stimulating his complaint gland. There was nothing left but to go home. To Audrey.

Audrey Philpot Grimes Newman Fisher.

Hal often told people that his wife had not been divorced twice; husband Grimes had died of a heart attack while going over her checkbook.

Audrey was the reward of every Jewish boy made good, the cherry syrup in his Coke, the extra slice of pickle with his hot pastrami sandwich, the shiksa goddess who made people stare at him and ask who he was. She was also, after eleven years of fruitless marriage, the olive pit in his salad Niçoise, the extra vermouth that kept his martini from being dry, the one to whom nothing, not even the triple crown of Emmy/Writers Guild/Humanitas awards was enough. Not, of course, that he'd ever won them.

But he did love her, still, in his stubborn, obstinate, and profoundly foolish way. It was his perpetual fantasy that one day he would write something so pure, so beautiful, so overwhelmingly human, that she would turn to him and love him the way he needed to be loved.

It had not yet happened.

The taxi moved up Amsterdam Avenue, behind the Met, past two police cars and an ambulance, a body covered with a yellow plastic tarp, and the curious held back by the police, then turned toward Central Park West and the row of proud cooperative buildings.

Mingus, who had been doorman at the Ed Sullivan Theater in the days of Topo Gigio and Señor Wences, now worked the door of Hal's co-op. He opened the cab door and, seeing his favorite tenant, burst into a gleaming prosthetic smile.

"How'd the taping go, Hal?" he asked.

"God bless the man who invented the laugh box."

"Not on your show, Hal."

Mingus began or ended every sentence with Hal's name. It was his due. He was seventy to Hal's fifty and, more important, a show biz comrade. He scurried from the cab to the front door ahead of his comrade, barely grasping the doorknob first. Mingus disliked it when tenants, especially important show biz tenants, tried to open the door for themselves.

" 'Night, Mingus."

" 'Night, Hal," and he closed the door, pleased that one more of his charges was home safely.

Audrey Philpot Grimes Newman Fisher was not at home. Hal vaguely recalled some reason why she couldn't come to the taping. Masseuse, aerobics, ballet, theater, opera, the day before her period, the day after her period, it was all the same. He reminded himself that she could always see the episode, edited and tightened (so that Glenda looked as if she knew what she was doing), on TV.

He made himself a drink and couldn't help but think of his mother in their days in the Bronx and her possessive fascination with his father's job in the pajama game. But his mother had a deviated septum and not a diploma from Radcliff. It was his Louis Quinze four-poster and he had to lie in it.

It was after two when Audrey slid into bed next to him. He had been asleep, but he woke partially to welcome her. And then he caught the scent of secretions and soap. The scent of Audrey Philpot Grimes Newman Fisher after sex.

His eyes burned when he closed them.

At any other gym in the city, Audrey Philpot Grimes Newman Fisher would have stood out as an example of what might be achieved through proper exercise, diet, and accumulation of wealth. But at Joan's Women she was not extraordinary, for Joan, the owner of the club, the cool, slender, and elegant doyenne of fitness, had her standards and these were rigid. The club was small, and the privileged few who were permitted to join came not to alter their bodies, but to glory in them. To be sure, there was a smattering of cellulite-marred thighs, an occasional love handle, even a dropped bosom or two, but for these imperfect few, what they lacked in physicality they made up for in wealth.

In the mirrored, velvet-draped aerobics room, manicured fingers encircled with diamonds and emeralds reached for the ceiling; bodies used to the touch of silk and fur swayed to the music; and all the while the masseuses and pedicurists and makeup artists awaited them in peach-colored cubicles.

The singers to whose music they danced were exclusively female. Donna Summer was warning all that "she works hard for the money so you'd better treat her right" when Joan entered the room. There was always a sudden intake of breath when she showed herself. Women of beauty and power reached higher, bent lower, tried to force out the perspiration to impress her. On this particular afternoon, she stood in the doorway, eyeing them as one inspects a tray of yellow diamonds for the fraudulent citrine. She was of no distinct age, presumably because, having lived through many ages, she had conquered all of them. Her hair hung straight and wheat-colored to her earlobes, and these displayed three ruby buttons in one, two fire opals in the other. Her nose was long and scissor-sharp, her lips thin and unpainted. She wore a silver robe tied around the middle and sandals, and had the look of a high priestess.

Her gaze went around the room, past Audrey to a

stunning redhead who, high on recent accomplishments, danced with the fervor of success.

"Sheila?" she called out in a stage whisper.

The redhead was waved out of the room with the priestess. Ten minutes later she returned, glowing and ebullient.

Television Studio 104 stood on Broadway at 55th Street in mute testimony to the lingering illness of that most fabulous of all invalids, the theater. It had once been a legitimate house, but now, on the stage where young Helen Hayes had first been admired by playwright Charles MacArthur, a group of builders and painters was erecting a bank—or, more exactly, the corner of a bank. In five days, Glenda was to sit at a desk in that corner, locked in mortal combat with a bank officer over how much she had or didn't have in her account. The stage of 104 was large and housed both the permanent set (living room, kitchen, bedroom, hallway) and whatever else might be needed for the weekly twenty-three-minute playlet (bank, prison, market, hospital). These extra sets were seldom complete; a corner, a backdrop wall, an entrance would usually do. If more was required, the writers were chastised by one of the army of producers about their wanton wastefulness. Even so, each episode of *Family Business* cost more than $400,000.

Downstairs, beneath the hammering and sawing noises, lay a rabbit warren of rooms: the editor's office, which smelled of cigars and cheeseburgers; the audience bathrooms, generally tidy but never clean; rooms for costumes, makeup, the herding of extras

12

until they were needed; dressing rooms for the cast, for guest stars; and the green room.

It was this last room that Hal entered the following Monday morning at ten. Each week started with a reading of two scripts: the current and the following weeks' episodes. The actors read the first hungrily, hoping to find new jewels for themselves, new jokes, new excuses for close-ups. As for the following week's script, they were always suspicious. What was it about? *Who* was it about? Would Glenda be its central character, or one of the children, or (most unlikely of all) *the husband?* It was rarely about *the husband,* for his popularity was limited and his agent was Glenda's agent and 10 percent of Glenda meant one never rocked the boat unless she requested it. For Glenda to request the enlargement of another actor's part was several degrees more farfetched than total nuclear disarmament under Ronald Reagan.

As he entered, Hal's glance fell on Betty, who sat at one end of the large table that accommodated actors, writers, director, and whichever of the producers succeeded in elbowing out his compatriots. The rest of the assemblage (set and costume designers, editor, and the losing producers) was banished to couches around the periphery of the room.

"You look awful," Hal said, taking the seat next to Betty. "Don't you sleep anymore?"

"What're you talking about? I got three hours last night. I'm practically a sloth."

"Have you ever thought of seeing a doctor?"

"I see Marcus Welby every night. At two A.M. I got you a bagel before they were all gone."

Hal looked down at his place at the table to see two scripts, one cup of coffee, and a dry bagel.

"No butter?"

"Marcus says cholesterol is bad."

"Cream cheese?"

"Marcus says you're too fat."

"Are you sure you're not Jewish?"

"I'm too tired to be sure of anything."

Hal picked up the naked bagel and crossed to a table at one end of the room that held two coffee urns, a bowl of fruit, and a platter of bagels and danishes. He was layering on the butter when Glenda spotted him and, in mid-conversation, hurried toward him. His peripheral vision warned him, and he was reminded of something he'd said to Stu years before: that, except for certain subspecies of rodents, Glenda was the only mammal that could smile and scowl simultaneously. And there it was. That hail-fellow-well-met grimace that passed for charm among the yokels.

"Hal, I've been thinking . . ."

He resisted delivering one of a hundred rebuffs that ranged from "With what?" to "I'll alert the media."

". . . you know that scene in the bank?"

"Yes?"

"Wouldn't it be funnier to drop the next scene at home and expand the bank part? I mean, it's the best thing in the show . . ."

Hal arranged his face to stimulate thoughtful consideration of the idea while remembering that the scene to be cut did not involve Glenda but rather *the husband*.

". . . and at the end I could make an impassioned plea against bureaucracy and red tape and the helplessness of the ordinary person against the system."

"Sounds like a million laughs." He decided what the hell, and added cream cheese on top of the butter.

"I'm not saying the words, just the gist."

"I'll think about it."

"Seriously?"

"Like it was cancer." It killed him that she was probably right.

"What did she want?" Betty asked without looking up from her script as Hal sat down next to her.

"To do a one-woman show."

Hal glanced around at the chatting, eating, gossiping, complaining group to see if the reading might start.

"Where's Scott?" The show's teenage son was missing.

"Outside calling his pusher."

Hal smiled. He loved it when Betty was bitchy. He felt a deep sense of pride, for when the funny-faced, thirty-four-year-old arrived in Gotham, via a sunny childhood in Tacoma, Washington, she had been incapable of the slightest rudeness. A few more months and he'd have her saying "fuck."

By the time Scott returned, two other cast members were in the john, the guest star was on the phone with his agent, two network executives had begged off for other meetings, and Betty was half-asleep.

Eventually, with great difficulty, the reading commenced. Glenda read every line with her mouth full of a succession of danish, banana, and orange, and her lines sounded slightly better that way. The other cast members were more distinct in diction but less spirited. Everybody had somewhere else they longed to be. Three years on a hit show, and they all condescended to it. After all, Meryl Streep and Dustin Hoffman didn't have to do a weekly show for their millions. It was unfair.

The reading of the second script was lackadaisical, sloppy, and constantly interrupted by actors who had drifted off and had to be elbowed back to the script. It was impossible to time the episode, the chief reason for the reading.

"Come, children," Hal summoned Betty and Andy when the internment was over. "Upstairs. We have one-liners to steal."

The writers' suite was on the third floor of Studio 104. One could, if one were retired or catatonic, wait for the elevator. Otherwise, one walked.

Betty and Andy, being young and annoyingly in shape, bounced up the stairs ahead of Hal, who bitched about looking four months pregnant.

"Stop putting butter on your bagels," Betty called back over her shoulder.

"Andrew, tell your friend to shut up."

"Shut up," Andy said obligingly.

Two hours later, Hal had written an eight-page scene that had two surefire showstoppers and a handful of possible laughs in it. He stretched his arms out in front of him and bellowed a yawn.

"Shut up in there, I can't concentrate," Betty called out from her office.

"How many pages have you written?" Hal called back.

"None of your business."

"I'm going to start paying you by the word, like Dickens."

"In that case, anybody know six words for 'infallibility'?"

"Could you two please be quiet?!" hollered Andy, prostrate on the floor of the reception area. "Some of us would like to be alone with our writer's block."

"I hate writing." This from Betty.

"I hate show biz," Andy responded. "Except maybe for bondage movies."

"I hate tuna fish." Hal this time. "Unless it's got a lot of mayo and onions. Anybody want to go to lunch?"

The phone rang before they could. Andy got it while Betty searched for one of her shoes and Hal went to the can. When he emerged, Andy was standing there, beaming.

"Look how happy he is just because I peed," Hal said to Betty. "Why can't you be nice like that?"

"We won an award," Andy said. "From Women in Media."

"Yeah? For what?"

"For depicting women in a positive and respectful way."

"Just because Glenda's flat-chested?"

"There's a dinner next week."

"Please." Hal waved it away. "Another Golden Tampon Award. You two go."

"Jacqueline Bisset is handing out the awards."

"We'll all go."

3

Ten minutes after the man entered the dimly lit singles bar, he struck gold. This was in the form of a fantastically attractive blonde who sent him a drink via the bartender. Such a thing had never happened to him before. This was a night to be savored and relived in memory and story.

Or was it a mistake?

He smiled at her, acknowledging the gift. She smoldered back. It was no mistake.

They talked about the stock market dip, upswing, and fall as if they were discussing a yuppie dance. She was informed, credible, and, most important, busty.

He finally summoned up his courage. "I'm going to say something and I hope I don't offend you."

"What?"

"Would you come home with me?"

She didn't like his apartment; it was glass and steel and one shade of gray, like a submarine in the sky. After a round of martinis and an awkward but nevertheless interesting talk about closed-end funds, she suggested they go to bed.

He nearly clapped his hands in his enthusiasm.

*   *   *

Later, lying there naked, exhausted, and humiliated because the blonde was the more sexually erudite of the two, the man remembered that he hadn't changed the message on his telephone answering machine since he'd gotten back to town.

"Excuse me," he said, leaning across her to the far side of the bed. "I've got to change my message."

As he pressed the replay button, his elbow dug sharply into one of her breasts.

"Ow!"

"What?"

"My breast."

He moved his arm quickly. "Sorry." Clumsy and sexually inadequate. No wonder things like this had never happened to him before, he thought.

"Hi, this is Merv and I'm at 203–868 . . ." the message started.

He climbed over her to be closer to the microphone, and his knee came down on her hand.

"Jesus!" she exclaimed.

He nearly fell over in his hasty attempt to release her crushed fingers.

"I'm really sorry."

"Please leave a message at the tone . . ."

"That's all right. I'll just get out of your way." She slid to the far and presumably safe side of the bed, but her long golden hair trailed behind, and in rearranging himself, he sat on it.

"I call in for them. Ciao."

"Excuse me, Herb?" she said.

"Merv," he corrected her.

"Merv, you're on my hair."

He leaped up. "I don't know what the hell is wrong with me tonight."

"It's no big deal."

"You're really nice," he said, and then, remembering that really nice women are seldom world-class sodomites, he blushed and hit the record button.

"Hi, it's Merv. I'm somewhere out there in the city now—"

She coughed, and the machine recorded it.

"Please?" He held his index finger to his mouth.

"Oh, sorry."

"I'll have to wait until the end of the tape. It's thirty seconds."

"I am sorry."

"Don't be silly. It's not your fault." They exchanged polite smiles as if they had just collided in a doorway rather than a bed.

As the tape droned on, they remained silent, she staring at her long, carmine-stained nails, he at his flaccid penis.

The droning stopped.

"I'm going to record now."

"I'll be quiet."

"Thank you."

He pressed the record button again. "Hi, it's Merv. I'm somewhere out there in the city now, so please leave a message at the tone. If you're calling for Anna, she's in Europe till the third. Thanks for calling, and please wait for the tone."

He quickly held his finger to his mouth again, to

indicate that the machine was still recording. She nodded and remained silent.

At the sound of the beep, they spoke simultaneously.

"I'm sorry," she said.

"No, what did you say?" he insisted.

"I asked who Anna was."

"Oh." His face dropped guiltily. "My wife."

"Yeah, I thought so."

"Are you married?" he asked.

"Yes, of course."

"Of course."

Later, when they were dressed and he had all but broken one of her toes by stomping on it in his cowboy boot, he suggested they have a nightcap on the terrace. It was dark enough so that no one would see that the woman with him wasn't Anna.

The woman who *was* with him looked down over the edge of the terrace into the back alley nineteen stories below. There was a dumpster, filled with debris from some remodeling project.

"Thank you very much," he said after an oppressive silence.

"You're welcome," she answered. And then, "Come here. I'd like to thank you, too."

He did, and proved so clumsy that it took no strength at all to push him over the railing.

He landed, appropriately she thought, in the dumpster.

4

On the evening of the Women in Media dinner, Hal got back to the apartment at five to change. Mingus, questioning him about his early arrival, was delighted.

"What is it, Hal? Like an Emmy?"

"No, it's just a little plaque from a women's group and some creamed chicken."

"Yeah? Terrific, Hal. Is that where Mrs. Fisher went, all dressed up?"

"I don't think so."

He knew it wasn't. Audrey had already given her excuses. All the way up to the apartment in the elevator, he tried to remember what those excuses were but couldn't. That was the way it was with lies.

He opened his closet door and stared at his clothes as if they belonged to someone else. What could an observer tell about the man who wore them? First, he made what his mother would have called "a good living." A very good living, judging by the labels. He was a 40 short with a thirty-six-inch waist, which meant he sat in good restaurants too often and drank too much. He had no children to keep him home at night, this man with all the sports jackets. Nor was there any indication that he was particularly happy, if you judged by the somber colors of his wardrobe.

Hal suddenly felt sorry for the man in the closet, and he grabbed his tuxedo and closed the door.

He made himself a drink, called his sister in Pennsylvania, and listened to her troubles; then, noticing the time, he begged off and got dressed.

Shit. The middle button of his tuxedo jacket was hanging loose. One's dress is inversely proportional to one's achievement, he thought; novelists and playwrights can be shabby, but the world expects its gagmen to be natty. He went in search of needle and thread.

Audrey's closet revealed nothing more than the fact that his wife spent more on clothes than *Family Business* did on all its regulars, guest stars, extras, and under-fives put together. Her shoes, lined up in perfect parallel symmetry, exhibited an anal retentive propensity. But even those gave no indication of what lay in store in Audrey Philpot Grimes Newman Fisher's dresser.

Top drawer, right: French linen handkerchiefs, some monogrammed, some not, and by the look of them, none had ever encountered the nose of Audrey P-G-N-F, let alone lowered itself to be used as a receptacle of any kind.

Top drawer, left: gloves. Leather, lace, cotton, lizard, black and blue, white and beige, long, mid-length, short. Hal remembered his mother's gloves. She'd had two pairs. One was black, for "going out," the other rubber, for cleaning the oven.

Top drawer, center: jewelry. Not the good stuff.

The good stuff was in a safe deposit box. He'd come a long way from the days when he kept his money in a NesCafé jar at the back of his closet so his sister couldn't "borrow" any.

He opened the carved jewelry box that nestled in the drawer, still hunting the elusive needle and thread. None. He lifted the inner tray. Nothing but a piece of paper, carefully folded in two and then in two again.

He read it.

Dalton Phillips, 1421 Park Avenue, NYC
Samuel Friedman, Central Park South, NYC
Mervin Johanssen, 5 East 62nd Street, NYC
Brendan Bacall, Greenwich, Ct.
Simon Woodward, 1440 Fifth Avenue, NYC
Ernst Goodman, 15 East 68th Street, NYC

He folded it, twice, and put it back in the jewelry box. Then, without thinking, he tore the offending button off his tuxedo jacket and left the apartment.

"What's the matter?" Betty asked him. They were seated at a small table with Andy and one of the associate producers from the show.

"What makes you think something's the matter?"

"When they announced that Jacqueline Bisset wouldn't be here, you were the only man in the room who didn't burst into tears."

"I don't like women," Hal answered, only half kidding.

"Then I'd say you're in the wrong place."

Betty was right. Of the two hundred people in the

24

hall, only fifty-odd were men. They sat in a sea of overachieving women, trying to remember not to pull chairs out and not to stand when someone approached the table.

"At least it's not creamed chicken." Betty smiled at him, indicating the prime ribs on their plates.

"Only dykes should serve prime rib."

Betty's smile faded. "That's not funny. Something *is* the matter."

"Yeah," was all he said.

The lights started to fade in the hall, and a woman Hal recognized as the reigning queen of nighttime soap opera writers stepped up to the podium.

". . . And for the humor and gentleness of their writing . . ."

After two hours of awards and speeches, Hal's sherbet, along with his disposition, had liquefied, one from the heat, the other from several gin and tonics. In front of him, in the center of the table, stood a Lucite globe mounted on a cube of mahogany that bore the show's name and the year. He sat, chin in hand, staring at it. And then a burst of applause from the audience roused him. He slapped his hands together enthusiastically and shouted, "Brava!" Then he turned to Betty. "Who won?"

She smiled at him sadly. "You want to take a walk with me outside?"

"Why?"

"Because it's warm in here."

"And because I'm drunk, right?"

"Right."

"Okay."

They got to their feet, Hal with a little help from Andy on his other side, and left. But not before Hal shouted one more *brava,* this in the middle of the recipient's acceptance speech.

They walked west from the Hilton to Eighth Avenue, then down Eighth into the Forties. The fifth time Betty asked him what was the matter, he turned to her and said, "I'm sorry. I wasn't raised to think of you as someone to talk to. I was raised to think of you as someone to fuck."

The bluntness of his response took her by surprise, and her eyes filled with tears.

"I'm sorry," she said.

"What're *you* sorry for?"

"For prying . . . I don't know. . . . Look, if you're okay now, I have to go home."

His head had cleared sufficiently for him to hear the hurt in her voice, and he studied her face. She was pretty, not much more. Her eyes, bright hazel and usually full of mischief, were avoiding his. And her lips, her best feature by virtue of their fullness, were trembling slightly at the ends.

"I'm drunk," he said simply.

"I know," she whispered, looking at the ground.

"What happened was—"

"Please." She stopped him. "It's none of my business."

"Yes, it is. You're my friend, so it is."

She thought for a moment, and the sadness gave way to a feisty resolve. "Damn right. I'm your friend, so let's have it. You've had a fly up your nose all night."

He smiled at her. So damn cute. "The expression is 'a fly up your ass.' "

"Not on TV at eight o'clock," she said, reminding him of their time slot.

"Okay." He took her arm as they walked past a teenager who was sleeping in a doorway. "I think my wife is having an affair. Shit, I *know* my wife is having an affair. I *think* she's having it with a god-damn brokerage house, judging by their addresses."

After he'd told her about the list, Betty silently assessed what she'd heard. Then, nodding vigorously so that her curly brown hair bounced along her shoulders, she said, "No, the truth is you don't know anything of the kind. You *think* it, that's all. But you're the one who thinks Audrey is too good for you, so what d'you know?"

"Then what could it be?"

"It could be anything. A list of her cousins on her mother's side. A list of her doctors—"

"Yeah, her gynecologists," he grumbled.

"Hal, for crying out loud." Betty turned him around so that they were face to face. "Who makes a list of their lovers? With their *addresses*? It's crazy!"

"She's very well organized. You should see her shoes." He smiled weakly, despite himself. "So what d'you think it is?"

"What're you asking me for? Ask Audrey."

"I'm asking you because I'll believe what you tell me."

"A man should believe his wife," she said sadly.
"Yeah. And Glenda should get her lines right."

He almost did ask Audrey. The following morning he came out of the bathroom to find her sitting up in bed, remote control in hand, watching the morning news. She had opened the blinds, and sunshine lit up her still sleepy face. Christ, she was beautiful, he thought. What man, what army of men, wouldn't want her? Of all her incredible features—the round, pale blue eyes, the pouting lower lip, the hair the color of his mother's powder puffs—the one that left him limp with awe and lust and wonder was her Ava Gardner/June Haver/Grace Kelly nose. From whatever angle you looked at it, it pointed gently upward, not abruptly upward like the pug noses of Susan Hayward or Kathryn Grayson, but *gently,* proud and fine, thin and regal, a nose of quiet dignity that had no ancestors in Russia, that had never smelled chicken fat frying in the pan, that might turn red at the edges with illness but never ran or dripped or sniffed or gave offense. God, he thought, what is it with Jews and noses?!

"You're staring at me," she said in a throaty, filled-with-sleep voice.

"I'm entitled. I'm your husband."

She didn't respond; she turned to the TV set, cutting him out of her line of vision. He hesitated, trying to form the words that would best allow her to lie about the list, that would give him another week or month or year before the coldness and the infidelity had to be dealt with. But he wasn't up to it, and so he left the apartment and was permitted to go without a word.

*   *   *

Hal could hear Betty and Andy's laughter from the stairwell before he entered the writers' office. They were stretched out on chairs in the anteroom, having a high old time.

"Okay, what's going on here?" Hal growled as he crossed to the coffee machine. "You think I brought you here from L.A. to have a good time? Let's see a little angst here. All right, where's my whole-wheat bagel? Which of you two brats ate my whole-wheat bagel?"

"There was none."

"Eat the poppy-seed bagel."

"I can't eat a poppy-seed bagel." He crossed into his office and went to the phone. "Whole wheat is roughage. My intestinal tract is half a century old. I have to take care of it." Then, into the phone, he said, "Phyllis, put down your horoscope and pick up."

"Yeah?"

"Don't yeah me. Where's my whole-wheat bagel?"

"Oh, shit, I forgot to tell them again."

"Thank you, Phyllis." And then, after a short pause, "Phyllis?"

"I'm sorry. Phyllis is dead. She just shot herself."

"Did she get any whole-wheat bagels before she did it?"

Phyllis laughed and clicked off.

"So, what are you two so happy about?" Hal asked as he crossed to the poppy-seed bagel and regarded it with disdain.

"It was either laugh or cry, and we cry enough about our private lives," Andy answered.

"Glenda's done it again."

"I don't want to know." Hal buried half the poppy-seed bagel under a slab of butter. "What?"

"She can't work the week of the twelfth."

"Why not? Life-threatening surgery, one hopes?"

"Stop that," Betty whined. "You don't wish her any harm."

Hal said to Andy, "Your partner's written too many children's shows. So? Why can't she work?"

"Because," and Andy started to laugh again, "she entered her Lhasa apso in a dog show and she's gotta be there to hold its paw."

"And that means we've got to work the week of the nineteenth, when I have a nonrefundable ticket to go to London for the first time in my life, and this is the third time Glenda's done this to me, but who's complaining?" Betty bit down hard on her own dry bagel.

"I told you over and over again," Hal said, stroking her hair, "make shoes for a living, not jokes."

"Before you get too philosophical about it," Betty said, "the episode we were supposed to do on the twelfth we can't do on the nineteenth because our guest star isn't available, so guess which three pixies have to come up with a brand-new script overnight?"

Later that afternoon, while working on the new script, Hal realized that in all his daydreams in which Glenda was wiped out, her face was Audrey's.

He had to know what the list meant. Dangerous though it might be, foolish though it certainly was, he had to know.

Questioning Audrey was useless, for even if she told him the truth, he wouldn't believe her.

How, then?

Betty entered his office and placed four sheets of paper on the desk in front of him.

"Read this and tell me you still believe I should write for a living."

He read through the pages quickly. "Good. Fine."

"Good? Fine? You didn't smile once!"

"I'm sorry. I'm not in the mood to smile."

"It's that stupid list, isn't it?"

"Yeah."

Betty went around behind his chair and, putting her arms around him, leaned her head on his. "I wish you'd forget it."

"I can't. I feel like I'm starving to death and I don't know why nobody'll feed me." He inhaled the scent of her hair. "You smell nice."

"Thank you. So do you."

"Naw. I smell like an old Jew."

She released him. "I hate when you do that."

"Do what?"

"Talk about yourself like that. You're not old, and Jew doesn't mean what you think it does."

"What do I think it means?"

"Unattractive, unworthy, the goddamn comic relief." He looked up and saw that she wasn't kidding. "It makes me so damn mad. I hate antisemitism."

"I'm not antisemitic. I'm anti-me."

"I hate that worse."

He smiled at her. "You're such a nice girl, you know?"

"No, I'm not," she answered. "I've got a fat ass, I'm not pretty, and I like Jews."

"You're right. You're fired," and he kissed her cheek, which was warm and flushed.

Hal sat alone in the living room of his apartment later that evening, having a third gin and tonic and surveying the evidences of his success. A mahogany baby-grand piano without a fingerprint on it sat in front of a Venetian glass mirror. A bronze Anubis, the Egyptian jackal, smirked from atop a marble pillar in the corner, lit by one carefully placed spotlight. The couches and chairs, covered in matching Clarence House flamestitch, made a tight room within the room, meant for lingering conversations with good friends. The fabric was as new and unworn as when Audrey selected it, two years before.

And where was the house-proud mistress of all this upward mobility? Out doing God-knows-what with God-knows-whom.

"Audrey, you're not a nice person," Hal called out to the empty room. "Or maybe I'm not a nice person. But someone sure as hell isn't nice around here!"

He went into the bedroom, opened the center drawer, the jewelry box, the list.

Dalton Phillips, 1421 Park Avenue, NYC.

He went to the phone and dialed information. Dalton Phillips's number was, at the request of the customer, unlisted.

He went back into the living room and sat on one of the couches, the wing chair, the piano bench, the windowsill.

What would he have said to Phillips if he had reached him? *"Hello, you don't know me, but I think you're banging my wife."* *"Hello, I'm Audrey Fisher's soon-to-be-ex-husband . . ."*

The thought stunned him. It was perhaps the first time he had, in any way, considered divorcing Audrey. It made him feel a little queasy, or maybe it was the gin. *Divorced.* Living alone. Sleeping alone. Dating. He thought of Stu and his constant complaint that all the souvenirs of his life were spread out among ex-wives. Hal grinned. There were things in this very room that marked the life of Newman, his predecessor in Audrey's marital conga line.

"Ma," he whispered. "What the fuck should I do?"

"First, don't talk dirty." he could hear his mother's voice as clearly as if she were standing next to him.

"All right, I'm sorry."

"You should be. If I had been alive, you wouldn't have married her so fast in the first place, believe me."

"I believe you."

"You should have married that other one. That one I liked."

"That one I didn't like," Hal answered. "There was no chemistry."

"Don't give me chemistry." She sounded like she had when he'd tried to pull the wool over her eyes about cutting a class or failing a test. *"I'm not interested in chemistry. I'm interested in your doing what's*

33

right. You married her for better or worse, am I right?"

"You're right."

"So you'll keep your mouth shut and you'll let sleeping dogs lie. You'll bring her some flowers, you'll be nice to her, everything'll be all right."

Sure, everything'll be all right, he thought. Like you won't get a heart attack from your damn cigarettes, and Papa won't waste away from cancer, and I won't be so alone that I marry her in the first place.

The next morning, lying in bed next to his wife, Hal made up his mind. If Audrey was having an affair, he would forgive her. The two of them would work through it together. If she was having *an* affair. If, on the other hand, she was shtupping a regiment, it would take three of them to work it through: him, her, and her psychiatrist, for surely that meant she was a nymphomaniac and that was a disease, not a choice. He rolled over and looked at her. She was frowning in her sleep. Why not? he thought. She's got a lot to frown about.

He got up to shower, and Audrey rolled over and covered her head with his pillow. He didn't know what time she had gotten in the previous evening, but he doubted that she'd be up before he left.

He showered.

Then, coming back into the room and hearing her little snores, he went to her dresser and withdrew the list.

Dalton Phillips, 1421 Park Avenue.
1421 Park Avenue.

1421 Park Avenue.

What he did when he got there was anybody's guess.

Walking across Central Park to the East Side, Hal encountered many mothers and nannies with their charges; there were dark little grandchildren of immigrants whose sneaker laces trailed behind them, ebony beauties with dazzling smiles who resisted all attempts at restraint, towheads from Fifth Avenue whose ironed playsuits would soon attest to their desire to be as dirty as anyone else.

A familiar mood of shame overcame him. He was childless, not because of any physical lack, but because of Audrey's pharmacological hold on him. It was her body and therefore her choice. He was to remain a nonfather.

As was usual when this particular shame was upon him, Hal reminded himself of his success. And thinking of that success, mixed with the business at hand, he created a new TV series in his mind: *The Cuckold Show*. Each week a different man would confront his wife's lover. Blood would flow and tears would spout as America got its collective rocks off. A forty share. The merchandising alone would mean he'd never have to work another day as long as he lived. *Cuckold* T-shirts. *Cuckold* coffee mugs. *Cuckold* condoms (in one size; small).

The pilot episode: Tony comes home to find Angelina in the sack with the Domino's Pizza boy. He shoots them both through the head, finishes the pizza, and goes to confession.

Episode two: An English guy goes to visit his wife's lover. They're civilized, they talk, they find out they went to the same public school, they fall in love.

Episode three: A Jew from the Bronx gets to 1421 Park Avenue and . . . ?

"Can I help you, sir?" The doorman finally confronted the man who had been standing nearby staring at the entrance to his building.

"No, thanks," Hal answered, suddenly ashamed. "I'm waiting for one of your tenants."

"Would you like to wait in the lobby?"

"No, I'm enjoying the air."

The doorman, a professional, showed no sign of the suspicion he felt. "Would you like me to buzz up and tell—"

"No, thanks." Hal was sure he was blushing. "Tell you what you could do for me, though. Could you point out Mr. Phillips when he comes out? I'm a friend of a friend of his . . ." he faltered, feeling like an idiot, stumbling over his lies.

"Which Mr. Phillips?" The doorman abruptly dropped the polite smile.

"Dalton Phillips."

Now his face held a kind of pugnacious suspicion. "Dalton Phillips? Really?"

"Yes." Hal tried to smile but failed.

"Listen, you can wait if you want to, but I think we both know that Mr. Phillips isn't coming out." For the first time, the doorman's tone was rude.

"What do you mean? Why not?"

"Because he was electrocuted in his bathtub a month ago."

Since this was the day they taped *Family Business,* Hal was reprieved from spending the next eight hours brooding on Dalton Phillips's shocking death (no pun intended, he thought to himself). He gave his attention to the business at hand, the murder of this week's script.

He and his staff crossed the stage, where the warm-up man was mobilizing the audience with a mixture of old jokes and geographic fellowship:

"Let's hear it for everybody from the tri-state area! . . . And now a hand for our visitors from Texas! . . ."

Hal glanced at the audience, the usual three-thirty dress rehearsal crowd: some unemployed, some kids cutting school, a few from solar systems other than ours ("Let's hear it for our visitors from Alpha Centauri!"), the tourists, the stoned, the wretched refuse.

"If they get the Anna Freud joke, I'll eat my beanie," he whispered to Betty.

"Ours is not to entertain," she answered. "Ours is to educate," and she did a double take on a man in the audience who was wearing three sweaters.

The three of them marched into the small office at the end of the lobby and across from the control room that belonged to them during tapings, and immediately attacked the candy-covered coffee table.

"I get the Almond Joy." Andy's hand moved with the speed of a lizard's tongue, snapping it up.

Betty and Hal locked on to opposite ends of a Cadbury's chocolate bar.

"I'm your boss," he said.

"You told me I should help you lose weight."

"Help me tomorrow."

"No."

"Andy, grab her arms."

"Children," Andy announced, his mouth already filled with candy, "share and share alike, like nice television writers."

They did as he advised, and once the sodas were spoken for and distributed, they settled down to wait for the monitor to show something other than the leg of a chair and a square of faux parquet.

Presently, the warm-up man ran out of simulated cheer, Stu introduced the cast rapturously ("Ladies and gentlemen, one of the finest and most caring human beings it's ever been my joy to work with . . ."), Hal choked down a gag and another square of Cadbury's chocolate, and the show began.

The week's episode started with a confrontation between Glenda and the teenage hoodlum who portrayed her son.

"For crying out loud, look at Glenda's dress," Hal said. "Is she sneaking in her goddamn designer clothes again?!"

"Halston," Betty sighed.

"She's supposed to be an accountant's wife. What kind of accountant's wife wears Halston?"

"The kind who has a network to pay for it."

They watched the first scene silently, each writing down the mutilated lines, the missed cues, the jokes that worked (the *few* jokes that worked), the many that didn't, the boom shadows on the wall, the fuzzy focus, the tuft of Glenda's hair that stood up in the back and would make matching the same scene in the second taping impossible.

The scene ended with a robust laugh from the audience and a grateful sigh from Andy, whose joke had caused it. There was a costume change before the second scene. Time for the warm-up man to check on where the rest of the audience came from and for the three writers to insert some jokes that might work. They all studied their scripts.

"Page three," Betty started. "Instead of 'the last man I believed sat next to me in the third grade,' what about 'the last man I believed had the incubator next to mine'?"

"How about 'the last man I believed was Richard Nixon'?" This from Andy.

"How about 'the last man I believed was the last man I believed'?" Hal said.

"Usher," Betty murmured.

"What's that?" Andy asked.

Betty acted it out, cricking her finger to an imaginary usher. "Usher," she asked the space, "what does that joke mean?"

"Let's try the incubator," Hal said, writing it into the script.

"Why do you always like her jokes better than mine?" Andy pretended to pout.

"Because she has big floppy tits."

"You guys." Betty shook her head in mock disgust,

secretly pleased that Hal had noticed she had any kind of bosom at all.

They changed a reference to Ed Koch to a reference to Ivana Trump, shortened several punch lines, added an old stuttering joke they hadn't used in four shows, and threw in the towel.

Dalton Phillips. Hal's face darkened.

"What's the matter?" Betty asked.

"Nothing."

The warm-up man, heard through the monitor, was telling the same tired jokes in response to the same inevitable questions from the audience. (Inevitable because the questions were written on cards, and half of the cards had been written by the warm-up man as his audition for the job.)

"Are Glenda and Marie [her best friend on the show] married?"

"No, they're just good friends."

"How much does it cost to tape an episode?"

"With or without my salary?"

"Is the cameraman on camera one going with anyone?"

Dalton Phillips.

"Are you all right?" Betty had been staring at Hal.

"Define 'all right.' "

"You want a cup of coffee?"

"No." Hal's tone announced that no further discussion was welcome.

He was like that. Open and warm until some private pain hit and metamorphosed him into her boss. Betty had never known a relationship like this one.

But then, she had never been in love before.

No one knew but Andy, and they never spoke of it, in deference to its hopelessness. Hal was married. And even if that cold and barren marriage were to dissolve, Audrey would be replaced by another of her sort. Thirty-four-year-olds with "big floppy tits" and bigger behinds were never the choice of short, pudgy, funny men. Unfair but true.

The second scene started, preventing Betty from sinking into a comforting bath of self-pity. And now Glenda did what Glenda did best. She got tongue-tied. To the absolute delight of the audience, she tried the same line twelve times, and each time the words leaped about as if they had a consciousness of their own. The audience cheered every time she forgot a phrase or spoonerized a pair of words or looked helplessly at the camera, declaring in a baby voice, "Don't worry, I'll get it." The three writers were also enchanted. Briefly they forgot that beneath the desperation of her effort was a cool knowledge that each and every member of the audience would go home to tell their family and friends that Glenda Carpenter was a "real person," whatever that might be. It was the old Judy Garland ploy. Make the last note seem impossible, and when you belt it out, the people will cheer.

When she finally got it right, they did cheer, making the tape unusable, for cheering is hardly the response to a line said once.

An hour later the taping was finished, the script red-penned until it appeared to be bleeding, and Hal, Betty, and Andy reduced to their usual once-a-week state of resigned apathy.

Stu entered the room happily. "Pretty good dress, huh?" he said.

They stoned him with candy.

Dalton Phillips had died when the radio he was listening to accidentally fell into his bath. A month ago. Hal sat alone in the writers' office between taping sessions, trying to make sense of it.

Why would Audrey have a dead man's name on her list? Perhaps he hadn't been dead when she drew up the list; after all, Hal had just uncovered it. It might have been in her jewelry box for months.

Or, most optimistically, it might be nothing more than a reminder of her past, a kind of out-of-date little black book.

Was it possible, just possible, that nothing was wrong between them?

Hal was smiling as Betty entered, looking for her purse.

"I know something you don't know," she singsonged, ferreting around in the found pocketbook.

"What?"

"What'll you give me to tell?"

"The lack of a punch in the chops."

"Deal," she said happily. "Arthur just asked Andy on a date."

"Who's Arthur?"

"Arthur, the boom man that Andy's been salivating over all season! Isn't that nice?"

"Very nice."

"I told Andy that if they get married we'd chip in and get them a food processor. Andy's always wanted one." She withdrew a neatly rolled joint from her change purse.

"What's that?" Hal asked as she whipped it out of sight.

"Nothing."

"Elizabeth Lancing, do you smoke drugs?"

"No, Daddy. It's an old Lucky Strike. The name just wore off." Like a naughty child, she held it out for him to see.

"I haven't had grass in a year, I'll bet." He looked at it fondly.

"Wanna come down to the men's room and light up?" Betty offered.

The grass was old, harsh, and strong. The two of them stood leaning against the wall of the men's room, passing the joint, enjoying the sensation of being outrageous and slowly floating upward and hovering over Studio 104.

"You know what?" Hal asked.

After a minute, Betty answered, "What?"

"*What* what?"

"What *what* what? You said what."

"I said what?"

"Yes."

"God, that's funny," and they laughed.

The audience was being admitted now for the second taping, and one of them opened the door, saw Betty, and froze.

"I'm sorry," Hal said, bleary and charming, "we're having a gangbang in here. You'll have to come back later."

The man stared.

"Oh," Hal added, "the other guys are in the stalls."

The man left. Hal turned around to find Betty studying a urinal.

"They're pretty," she said. "You're so lucky. You have urinals and boxer shorts. All we have is PMS and yeast infections."

They were down to a roach, and Betty held it to Hal's lips for the last drag.

"Thank you," he said, grinding the butt into the tiled floor. "I needed that. Dalton Phillips is dead."

"Oh, my God, no," she cried. "And he looked so well!" And then she thought better of it. "Who's Dalton Phillips?"

"You know."

"I do?"

"Don't you?"

"Don't I what?"

"Don't you know who Dalton Phillips is?"

"Oh. I don't think so. I know who Dalton Trumbo is. And the Dalton School. And *The School for Scandal*." She got a fit of the giggles. When it subsided, she looked at him apologetically. "I'm sorry. I didn't mean that."

"You didn't mean what?"

"I didn't mean to laugh."

"You laughed?"

"Are you stoned?" They were red eye to red eye.

"Hello," he said, and kissed her gently on the lips. "What were you saying?"

"I didn't say anything. Did I?" Betty was thoroughly confused.

"Oh, no, it was me. I said Dalton Phillips is dead."

"Again?"

"Still."

"Wow." Betty's head cleared an iota. "Who's Dalton Phillips?"

"You know. The one on Audrey's list."

"Not that list again." She put her arms around his neck and went limp.

"Yes, that list again." Now he was holding her up. "What should I do?"

"About what?"

"The list!" he whined.

"You mean the list that the man who's dead is on?"

"Yes!"

She smiled, leaned her head on his chest, and closed her eyes.

"I know," Hal said through the haze in his brain. "I'll call the next guy on the list, that's all. Why didn't I think of that before?"

The men's room door opened and a network executive entered.

"Hi, John-Boy," Hal said, walking Betty out of the room.

Hal spent the second taping on an emotional elevator, stoned and fascinated one moment, depressed and sleepy the next. By the time he got home, he was vaguely nauseated and definitely out of sorts. Audrey was in the living room watching an old movie.

"Hi, Margaret, Betty, Bud, Kitten," he said sourly. "I'm home."

Audrey, who was used to him making inside jokes to himself, ignored it. "You hungry?" she asked.

He recalled how ravenous he'd been during the taping and, to his annoyance, the two and a half chocolate bars he'd eaten. "No, I ate."

"How'd the show go?"

"All right. Glenda got four lines right."

Audrey chuckled. "Which episode?"

"The one where her son won't date the girl because she isn't pretty."

"Oh, yeah, I read that one. I liked it."

It occurred to Hal that they were actually having a *conversation*. It also occurred to him that he had been starved for just this, but in his present chemically induced mood, he resented the wait more than he enjoyed the company.

"I'm beat. I'm going to bed," he said, leaving the room. "Good night June, Ward, Wally, Beaver."

Audrey said nothing.

In their bedroom, Hal went directly to her dresser. *Samuel Friedman, Central Park South.*

He copied it down on a slip of paper and put the paper in his wallet.

Tomorrow, he thought. Tomorrow I'll find out what the hell is going on.

And then, fully dressed, he stretched out on the bed and fell asleep.

5

The plump lady with the pavé rings was sitting in her Cadillac munching from a bag of Chicken McNuggets. On the dashboard, precariously placed, was a chocolate milkshake, and next to that a pack of More cigarettes and a package of Freedent gum. The radio played the theme from *Elvira Madigan,* which she'd once heard someone say was by Mozart. She thought it was pretty.

She was parked across the road from a heavily landscaped driveway, and she stared at it as she ate.

She averted her eyes from the driveway only once, to search the bag for more catsup packets. Finding none, she pouted and, to make herself feel better, thought of the lobster fra diavolo dinner her husband had promised her. With a baked potato, coleslaw, and Key lime pie.

She belched a very small, ladylike belch, practically a hiccup, and glanced at the car clock. Two-ten in the afternoon.

Soon. He had an appointment in Manhattan at four with his lawyer. He'd have to leave soon.

She remembered that the restaurant she and her

husband were going to that evening served string french fries. She debated whether to have them instead of a baked potato, but then a sense memory of the taste of baked potato with sour cream and chives made up her mind.

The music ended and a female announcer confirmed that it was indeed by Mozart, that the weather in southern Connecticut was fair and seasonably mild, and that there would be a tag sale for charity on Saturday at the football field of the local high school. She wondered how anyone could bear living in the sticks, all the really good restaurants being in town, not to mention the movies and department stores.

To pass the time, she tried to name her favorite stores that started with the letter *b*: Bonwit, Bendel, Bloomingdale's, B. Altman, Barneys, Balducci's . . .

His car came out of the driveway.

She quickly wiped her greasy fingers on a napkin from the McDonald's bag and turned the key in the ignition. The milkshake caught her eye. She hiked up her dress and placed the cool container between her thighs, wincing at the temperature. She put the car in drive and followed him.

They drove slowly through local streets, she half a block behind him, so there was time to light a cigarette and enjoy that first drag after food. There was even time to take a slug of milkshake before putting it back between her thighs and speeding up.

They were approaching the highway.

She was nervous but exhilarated. She hoped she wouldn't get the hiccups. She often did, from excitation after eating.

She was right behind him on the entrance ramp, so close in fact that she had to hit the brake to avoid bumping him. And that caused the cool milkshake to slosh on the warm insides of her thighs. Damn it, she would have a dozen oysters on the half-shell before her lobster fra diavolo. She deserved it.

He blended into the flow of traffic on the highway heading toward town, and she would have been right behind him again except for a Latin hooligan who refused to slow down.

She was in the lane next to his, two car-lengths behind. She sped up, tailgating the car in front of her, forcing it to pull off to the right.

Now there was one car-length between them, and she had absolutely made up her mind to a side order of french-fried onion rings and cream, not milk, in her coffee.

The car ahead of her also pulled off to the right, the driver intimidated by the woman who was so close he could see the end of her cigarette glow. She pressed on the gas pedal and pulled up alongside the man she was following.

Side by side.

She looked over at him. He glanced back. He was nice-looking. He reminded her of a waiter who had always been particularly nice to her and her husband whenever they dined at his restaurant. He always made sure their water glasses were full and her ashtray clean. She suspected he even put a few extra slices of the warm rye bread she liked in their basket.

She edged toward the right, closer to his car.

The brisket at his restaurant was marvelous. Never dry, like at other places, but juicy. And tender.

Closer.

And you could get nockeral, even though it wasn't, strictly speaking, a German restaurant.

He looked over at her. She was too close. He tapped his horn.

But the best thing, the absolutely best thing they served was the roast veal shank.

She moved closer, and it occurred to him that they might actually hit. He beat his horn now, but she still seemed to be getting closer.

And gravy! Such gravy!

Fortunately, the truck ahead of him moved one lane left, permitting him to accelerate and get away from the idiot woman driver with the screwed-up peripheral vision.

Several cars back, having lost him, the plump lady with the pavé rings promptly lost her appetite.

6

There were no Samuel Friedmans on Central Park South, but there were two S's and one S.J. Hal was about to dial the first when Andy walked into his office with the latest air-date schedule of episodes.

"Guess what?" he said.

"You and the boom man are in love."

"Who told—" Andy turned to the door and hollered, "It's impossible to have any privacy around here when your partner thinks she's the reincarnation of Louella Parsons!"

"Greetings from Hollywood," Betty called back in a fair imitation.

"They scheduled our two-parter with a preemption in the middle. See?" Andy pointed to the schedule.

"So, the audience'll have another week to worry about whether or not Glenda has an affair. As if anybody gives a shit."

"Please." Andy put his hand over his heart. "I'm trying to keep my morale up. We're not in the top twenty anymore."

"Sorry," Hal said. "The world is desperate to know whether Glenda will boff the visiting veterinarian."

"Thank you." Andy turned to leave.

"Or the visiting boom man."

Andy smirked. "Just don't ask what we do, okay?"

"I already know."

"How d'*you* know?"

"You're not the first gay friend I ever had, you know."

"Oh." Andy stopped at the door. "What do *you* guys do?"

"These days? Nothing."

"Sorry."

"It doesn't matter. The last time Audrey did anything to it, all that came out was a little dust, anyway."

Andy hooted and left, and Hal found the first S. Friedman's number in the phone book and dialed it. While he waited for someone to answer, it occurred to him he hadn't a clue what he would say if they did. On the fourth ring, it was answered.

"Hi. This is Suzanne. I'm not in now, but at the tone . . ."

He hung up. Down to two.

Before he could dial, Betty leaned in.

"A little *dust?* Poor old thing."

"Shut up and go away."

"Not until you stop making *old* jokes about yourself."

"Do you realize that if I hadn't matured so late, I'd be old enough to be your father?"

"My father's sixty-two and he doesn't get stoned with me in men's rooms and he doesn't talk about his genital functions in front of me."

"I didn't say anything in front of you. I said it in front of Andy and," he shouted at the door, "if he didn't run around repeating all my best lines, I would now be alone to make my phone call!"

"Who're you calling that's so important?" Betty asked.

Hal was suddenly ashamed of what he was doing. "My proctologist."

"Another *old* joke."

"Believe me, my asshole is no joking matter."

"You're so bad." She leaned across his desk and kissed his forehead. "Shall I close your door?"

"Please."

He turned back to the phone book and made call number two.

"Hello?" A live woman answered this time.

His throat seemed to close down. He swallowed and spoke. "Is this the home of Samuel Friedman?"

"Yes."

He thought he was sweating. "Uh . . . could I talk to him, please?"

"Who is this?" the woman on the other end asked.

"He doesn't know me. My name is—" Should he give his name? If he did, there'd be no backing down. He'd have to tell Samuel Friedman why he'd called, and it could, might, *would* get back to Audrey. "—Andrew Lancing," he said, mixing Andy and Betty and coming up with an alias.

"May I ask what this is in reference to?"

"Well," he *was* sweating, "it's kind of personal. I'd really rather speak to him directly."

"I'm sorry." The woman's voice remained calm and businesslike. "But perhaps if you could tell me what this is about, I could help you."

"Is this his secretary?" Hal asked because of her tone.

"No, this is his wife." And then, after the briefest of pauses, "His widow."

"What?!"

"My husband passed away a few weeks ago."

He sat there at his desk, making a list of his own: possible reasons why his wife had a list of rich men, the first two of whom had recently died.

She was making pin money by running a little funeral-related business on the side.

She was taking a writing course. Obituaries. It was a list of her homework assignments.

Old Audrey had turned necrophiliac and was lining up a few dates.

Why the hell didn't he just ask her?!

Because he couldn't.

He pressed the button on his intercom. "Betty, would you come in, please?"

Andy answered, "Me, too?" '

"No, just Betty."

She did, with a very odd expression on her face. "Am I in trouble?" she asked.

"No, I think I am."

"Oh. Let me calm Andy down. He's afraid you're mad at him."

"God, the paranoia around here," he said, and then laughed, thinking he might be the most paranoid of all.

Betty returned in a few moments, having assuaged Andy's upset over being left out. "What's up?" She pulled a chair up to Hal's desk.

"You know that list?" he started, half expecting her to throw up her hands in disgust and lecture him about the stupidity of his obsessive interest in a scrap of paper.

"Yeah?" She appeared honestly concerned, almost worried.

How he wished she had pooh-poohed it.

"The first two men on the list are dead."

She said nothing, just stared at him.

"The first was electrocuted in his bathtub, and the second was killed by a hit-and-run driver."

"What do you make of it?" she asked gently.

"I don't know."

"You're upset, though, aren't you?"

"Yeah, I think it's safe to say I'm upset. My heart is pounding like a set of bongos, I'm sitting here in a pool of sweat, and I might just wet myself for the first time in forty-six years. Yeah, you might say I'm upset."

She reached across the desk and took his hand in hers. "Can I say something without you getting mad?"

"What?"

"Remember when I first came here from L.A.? I was a wreck. New city, new job, new home. You sent me to a shrink and—"

"Betty, I don't need a shrink. I'm not imagining I saw that list."

"But you're imagining all sorts of crazy things about it. And the craziest thing of all is that you refuse to simply ask your wife what it is."

"I can't."

"Why not?"

He avoided her eyes. "It's too ugly to talk about."

"Try me."

"Audrey and I aren't exactly Charles and Di."

"Charles and Di aren't Charles and Di," she said.

"Yeah, but they can't get a divorce and we might. Audrey might force us to. If she does, I want some proof that . . ." He felt the shame ignite his face. "Look, I just don't want some judge taking the gold out of my molars and giving it to her. If that makes me a shit, I'm a shit."

He looked down. She was still holding his hand. Tightly. After a moment he allowed their eyes to meet. Hers were filled with tenderness and acceptance.

"Ain't love grand?" he said.

There was a homeless man sitting on a bench across the street from Hal's building when he got home. For a shocked moment, he thought he recognized him as a friend from the old neighborhood. Mingus held the door for him, but Hal had to check it out.

He crossed at the corner, to give himself a long enough walk toward the man to really see him.

He was dressed in an odd, comical assortment of cast-offs: gray suit jacket, tan vest, faded jeans ripped at the knees, brown cordovan shoes, and a kid's baseball cap that, being too small, was held in place with a large bobby pin. Hal saw his face in profile and again felt the shock of recognition. It was him. As a kid, he'd lived around the corner from Hal and his family. He'd been a pretty good stickball player, a great runner, probably to shut his mother up when she screamed for him at the top of her lungs. He had an older sister, the first bleached blonde in the neighborhood and consequently the first slut. She'd most likely been a virgin till her wedding night, but the hair defined her, as far as the neighbors were concerned.

What had happened to make him the one who sat on a bench in other people's clothes, and Hal the one who saw his name on TV every week?

With a wave of shame, Hal reached for his wallet. Yes, he had problems: a cold wife, a stupid accountant, a nemesis at the IRS, a co-op board that bled him for assessments—but what were these compared to what the real world lived with? What this man lived with?

He handed a dollar bill to the boy who used to play second base and had collected all the E.C. horror comics of the fifties.

It was somebody else. This other person took the dollar with a hostile look and pushed it into his vest pocket. Then he looked away, ignoring the big spender with the tragic look on his face.

Over dinner, Hal saw all the things about Audrey that he loved, and a few he hated. She had been out shopping and was still dressed to kill, her hair pulled back simply; she wore little makeup, and even that was superfluous. She was, in the vernacular of his childhood, *class*. The lady in the cashmere sweater at Gucci. The woman at the opening of the Impressionist exhibit. The one you let have the taxi even though you were there first.

"I thought we might drive out to see Muriel this weekend," Hal said, making his semiannual attempt at getting Audrey and his sister together.

"Fine, if you like," she said affably.

Fine? Since when? The last time he'd tried, he recalled Audrey saying something about boiling Mazola being preferable to an evening with Muriel and Norm.

"Great," he went on. "Maybe we should stay over. They have that nice new guest room."

"Why not?" Audrey pushed her dinner plate away, smiled, and lit a cigarette, all the while staring at him.

I'll tell you why not, he thought, returning the smile. Because even I wouldn't be caught dead in all that knotty pine.

"Good. I'll call her," he said.

"Good." She inhaled deeply and stopped smiling just long enough to blow the smoke out.

There they sat, showing each other all their available teeth, in a mockery of pleasantness. Hal hadn't seen such acting since they told Glenda that Steven Spielberg was in the audience. (He was—the audience of his wife's play, fifteen blocks away.)

Audrey served brownies and burnt almond ice cream for dessert, which meant she was either: one, hiding something; two, preparing to ask for something; three, preparing to hand him the bill for something; or, four, all of the above.

They chatted for a while, mostly about him (a dead giveaway that something was up). And then the phone rang and Audrey settled in for a long talk with her idol, a woman whose husband made money faster than she could spend it.

Hal went into the bedroom and got the list.

Brendan Bacall, Greenwich, Ct.
Simon Woodward, 1440 Fifth Avenue, NYC

THE LAST MAN ON THE LIST

Ernst Goodman, 15 East 68th Street, NYC
Harold Federstein, 1 East 87th Street, NYC
Malcolm Terrell, 124 Riverside Drive, NYC
Sidney Monroe, Glen Cove, L.I.

He stared at the list, not quite understanding what was wrong with it. And then it hit him. Dalton Phillips was missing. Samuel Friedman was missing. And somebody else was missing. Although he didn't remember the name, the address—5 East 62nd Street—had stuck. He'd once put in a bid on an apartment in that building.

This was a new list.

A list of men who were dead.

Or were they?

He knew that the first two had died accidentally, a fallen radio, a hit-and-run driver, but they had been taken off the list. Were the rest, then, also dead?

Or were they dying? Slowly. One by one.

He had started to shiver. He thrust the list back in the jewelry box, then opened his closet and reached for a sweater, but his hand moved quickly to a suede windbreaker.

He was going to 5 East 62nd Street.

The cab driver who sat in front of Hal on his latest odyssey was hardly more than a child. He appeared to be in his late teens, though, being Pakistani, he was probably older. He made no attempt at conversation with his passenger, which was just as well, for Hal was too preoccupied to engage in any.

Were the men being killed?

The question was answered without his asking it, for as the cab pulled up in front of 5 East 62nd, Hal saw the realtor who had almost sold him an apartment in it. She was talking animatedly with one of the doormen.

He paid the silent driver and got out. "Frances," he called to her.

She came up to him, all smiles, and leaned in close to study his face through thick, rhinestone-studded glasses. She showed no sign of recognition.

"Hal Fisher." He returned the smile.

"Don't tell me." She held her hand up, palm toward him. "I sold you an apartment in River House, right?"

"Wrong."

"Of course. It was the U.N. Plaza."

"It wasn't anywhere."

She leaned back and stared at him over the top of her glasses, as if that would jog her memory. "So what're you talking to me for if I never sold you an apartment?"

"You almost sold me one. Does that count?"

"Where?"

"Here." He pointed at the building. "A few years ago."

"Oh." Her smile returned. "You still looking?"

"Maybe." If he was to get any information from her, it occurred to him, he'd better be a prospective client.

"Because I have a beauty for you. Just went on the market." And she leaned in to whisper in the loudest whisper he'd ever heard, "The husband fell off the terrace and the wife is selling. Two bedrooms, full kitchen, a marble bath you could throw a dinner party in—"

"What was his name?"

"What was whose name, darling?"

"The husband who fell off the terrace?"

"How should I know? I never met him." Then she laughed. "Oh, you mean his *last* name. Johanssen."

Bingo. The third man on the list. The third one to die accidentally.

"Wait a minute! Call me! Take my card!" she yelled after him as Hal hurried away.

He was in a small bar on Lexington Avenue having his second martini. He stared into the glass, smiling in recollection of the day when, like a good Jewish boy, he'd have one white wine spritzer and drop his pants. That was before fame, fortune, and Audrey had hit.

What was she doing, his beautiful shiksa wife, with a hit list? If it *was* a hit list. There's always a possibility of another explanation, he reminded himself. Yeah? Like what? Like . . .

"One more," he signaled the bartender, and then, without knowing why, he started to mentally name all the people who were now dead that he might have turned to for help. Ma, Pop, his old friend Dennis (who'd dropped dead, literally, from aggravation), his Uncle Burton, who'd once told him his parents were full of shit. It was a small, select group, those people he trusted.

And then he remembered one who was still alive. Betty.

"I'm coming over," he said into the phone.

As she replaced the receiver in its cradle, it occurred to Betty that Hal had never seen her apartment; and, glancing around as if the same were true of her, she was appalled. Thirty-four years old, and she lived like she had just left her parents' home. Cast-off furniture filled the small studio, wicker next to faded chintz, bookshelves hastily made of planks of wood and bricks; my God, she even had Toulouse-Lautrec prints culled from a local junk shop.

And, most telling of all, a murphy bed.

The transience of her life was unmistakable, the rootlessness of a woman who refused to own permanent possessions, as if their purchase doomed her to be alone forever.

She could at least tidy up the naked truth.

In the bathroom wastepaper basket was a bunch of tired chrysanthemums. She pulled off the most withered and browned petals and returned the bouquet to an opalescent vase, one of the few purchases she had given in to. The lumpy needlepoint pillows she'd made one summer when she broke her ankle were fluffed and placed and replaced until they hid the worst stains on the couch. Remnants of several meals were swept away, half a dozen potted plants rearranged, half a dozen pairs of shoes tossed into the bottom of her closet.

Another appraisal of the room confirmed her suspicion that it was of no use. Hal would be there shortly and would know the worst.

Time for one more attempt to hide the truth. She hurried into the bathroom and studied her face in the mirror of the medicine cabinet. Oddly enough, she liked her face. Not that it was pretty or striking or even filled with character, but it was, as her mother had said ad infinitum, *sweet*. It was the face of someone who wished no one harm. That and a dollar-fifteen would get you a ride on the subway, she reminded herself.

She was halfway through applying fresh lipstick when the doorbell rang.

Hal entered, distraught, and looked around.

"Jesus, this is nice," he said.

She made him coffee and an English muffin with melted cheese on it. She listened to his story about the list of men who were being murdered, one by one. She heard his theories, which ranged from Audrey being a Mafia princess to the whole thing being a grotesque joke thought up by rival comedy writers. And finally Betty watched as he stretched out on her couch and fell asleep.

She sat down on the first piece of junk furniture she'd bought when she moved to New York, an old Morris chair, and watched him sleep. It had been a while since she'd seen him look this serene, this untroubled, and it would probably be a long time before she saw it again.

He was handsome, her friend, her boss, the potbellied fifty-year-old who lay there on her couch, snoring.

She had lied to him. She'd told him her father was sixty-two. He was fifty-eight. They might be friends, her father and this man. She went and got a quilt out of the closet and covered him. Then she sat down again and watched him in his sleep.

"I love you," she said to him quietly, and then she pulled down the murphy bed.

"Hey, boss, we're late." Betty was standing over him, her face scrubbed clean, her hair under a towel.

"Jesus Christ," he said thickly, "is that what you look like in the morning?"

"Pretty gruesome, huh?"

"No, I like it. You don't have any eyelashes."

"I will later. First I make coffee, then I make eyelashes."

Hal looked at his wristwatch. It was ten after ten. "Hey, we're late," he said, sitting up.

"Where have I heard that before?" Betty smirked, spooning coffee into a filter. "You want chocolate-covered doughnuts or sugared crullers? The dough-nuts are a week old. I think I brought the crullers with me from L.A."

"I'll wait for my whole-wheat bagel." How could such a wonderful girl eat such crap? he thought. Audrey wouldn't have that junk in the house.

Shit. Audrey. Like clouds rolling in from the horizon, the black thoughts returned as Hal's mind focused.

"Care to call my wife and tell her where I was all night?" Hal looked down at his wrinkled clothes. "Where's my suede jacket?"

"I hung it up."

"That's nice. You're a nice person."

"Hey." She bowed. "Winner of the Eleanor Roosevelt Award three years in a row. If it weren't for that tramp Mother Teresa, I would've made it four.''

He smiled for the first time in twelve hours. '' 'That tramp'? You're beginning to sound like me.''

"Well, you lie down with pigs." She handed him a glass of orange juice.

"Oh? Did you lie down with me?"

She looked away quickly so he wouldn't see her embarrassment. "Call your wife."

"Oh, God." He drained the glass. Fresh-squeezed. It had been a while since he'd tasted that. "Where's the phone?"

"Three inches below your chin." It was on the coffee table. "There's a long cord," Betty added. "So you can take it in the bathroom if you want privacy."

"Where's the bathroom?"

"You sure you don't want coffee first?" She pointed at the door. "You're not too bright this morning."

"Hey, I make up my best lies when I'm half-asleep." He went into the bathroom and closed the door.

Betty's smile faded. She felt a wistful thrill at being the reason Hal had to lie to his wife, even though it was a joke.

"Hello?" Audrey's voice was hoarse with sleep. So much for her staying up all night worrying, he thought.

"Audrey, it's me."

After a beat, she asked, "What time is it?"

"Ten-fifteen."

"Oh, no. Why didn't you wake me before you left? Now I'm late."

Before he left? He couldn't believe it. She didn't even know he hadn't been home.

"What do you want?" she snapped, obviously out of bed and running.

He smiled bitterly. "Take my gray slacks to the cleaners," he said, and hung up.

He put the top down on the toilet and sat down. He could feel himself filling with a new emotion, one he couldn't define at first. Somewhere in it was a sense of relief. He would no longer feel guilty for sneaking around behind her back, trying to find out what she was up to, he decided. He felt a burning in the pit of his stomach. It was probably the acid in the orange juice, he told himself. Or rage. Rage at having settled for so little over the years. For having endured a marriage that was sterile and left him starved for intimacy, surviving on crumbs of affection. Perhaps he didn't love the ice goddess at all; and even if he did, what did it matter? One could love the sea, but wading out into it still meant death. The truth that he faced, sitting there in his friend's bathroom, looking over her cosmetic bottles and inhaling the scent of her, was that he was going to divorce Audrey. He was going to start his life over.

All this because his wife didn't give a damn whether he came home or not.

But first, he promised himself, I will find out what the list is, and if I can use it against her to defend myself, I will.

He came out of the bathroom and said to Betty, "I've been a schmuck long enough."

"I'll drink to that." She toasted him with her coffee cup. "Any particular reason?"

He told her of his resolve to divorce Audrey and his new found resentment of her, and all the while she held her face as rigid as stone for fear of bursting into laughter or into tears.

He arrived at his apartment shortly after eleven to find Audrey gone and their twice-a-week cleaning woman in the kitchen ironing his shirts.

"Hey, Meg," he said, crossing to the coffee machine for another cup. "How are things?"

"Fine," she answered, beaming as always.

He knew that things were far from fine with her. Her eldest son was in constant trouble and her husband God-knows-where, but that was Meg's way, to smile and say "Fine" and keep her grief to herself. He always felt a little ashamed in front of her; she could make joy out of a tenth of what he had, and all he could make was despair.

"I saw the show last night," she said. "That woman is so funny."

"Yeah, Glenda's droll, all right."

"She has such a funny way of putting things."

"She's a real wit," he said, leaving the room. He had learned years ago never to explain that actors don't make it up as they go along, but he did wonder what Meg thought he did on the show.

In the bedroom, he retrieved the list and put it in his jacket pocket.

"I'll be back in a few," he called to Meg as he left.

In a half hour he returned, put the original list back into Audrey's jewelry box, and sat on the edge of the bed examining his photocopy.

He picked up the phone. "Information, I'd like the number of Brendan Bacall in Greenwich, Connecticut." After being briefly chastised for bothering a New York City operator with such an ignoramus's question, he was given the proper number to dial for that information. He did so, only to be told once again that the number was unlisted.

"What is it with these guys?" he murmured to himself, and redialed New York City information. "I'd like the number of Simon Woodward at 1440 Fifth Avenue." Having been a good boy this time, he was rewarded by a female computer reading off the seven digits. He dialed them.

"Hello?" a man answered.

"I'd like to speak to Simon Woodward, please."

"You are."

Hal froze.

"Hello?" the man said after a moment of silence. "Are you there?"

"Yeah, I'm still here." He was starting to hyperventilate. "Can I talk to you for a minute?" he forced out, trying to catch his breath.

"Who is it?" Woodward asked.

"I'm Audrey Fisher's husband." He felt dizzy, almost faint.

"I'm sorry. I don't know who that is."

Hal stared at the list. "Do you know a man named Brendan Bacall? Or Ernst Goodman?"

"No. Look, I think you may have the wrong person. I don't know any of them."

From his tone Hal could tell he was about to hang up. But he mustn't! He was the first man on the list who was still alive, and somehow it was up to Hal to warn him.

"Please," Hal started, "this isn't a crank call. I need to talk to you. I'll come to your place if you like—"

"No, I don't like." Woodward's voice had picked up a tone of discomfort. "Who *are* you?"

"My name is Hal Fisher. I write the TV show *Family Business*." Then he realized how insane that must sound.

"Wait a minute, I think I remember your name from the credits," Woodward said. "I'm sure I do. It's one of our favorite shows." Impressed, he became friendly.

Hal smirked. No matter how outrageous the lunatic, if he's in show biz, he's okay. Smile, *Candid Camera* just burned down your house.

"Look," Woodward went on, "I'm about to take our dog for a run in the park. If you'd like to meet me—"

"That'd be great. Great!"

They agreed to meet in the children's playground just south of the Metropolitan Museum. Before walking over there, Hal had time to shower, change, and try to think of what to say to the man so he didn't think he was out of his mind.

That would make one of them who didn't think so.

7

Simon Woodward looked like his Afghan hound; both were long and elegant, gaunt and aristocratic. But Shazam was entirely too aristocratic this afternoon. She refused to do her business no matter how Simon implored.

"For Daddy," he whined.

She sniffed at the ground. Nothing.

"Shazam, when we get home, you're not going out again until Mommy comes home from work, so you'd better do something."

She glanced at him and loped along at the end of her long leash, her ears and tail flouncing in disrespect for Daddy, who sighed and followed.

They were in the park at 72nd Street, heading down the hill to the wading pond where no one, not even Shazam, was permitted to wade.

Halfway down the hill, Simon heard a voice behind him.

"Oh, look, Trixie, look at the beautiful dog!"

He turned, assuming that the praise was for Shazam. He was right. A short, stocky woman was pulling a white toy poodle down the hill after her, trying to catch up to them. He smiled, pleased as always when strangers wished to make a fuss over his baby.

"Isn't he elegant!"

"She."

"I'm so sorry, *she*. Now, don't tell me she isn't a champion. She must be." Shazam leaned down to sniff her dog's genitals.

"She could be, I'm sure," Simon said, beaming, tugging ever so gently at Shazam's leash so that her nose found a more seemly spot to sniff. "But we never enter her. She's much too meek to subject her to that kind of pressure." Shazam found the poodle's anus.

"That is so considerate of you," the woman said, falling into step with him. "Most people have absolutely no regard for their pets' feelings."

They climbed down the hill quietly for a beat, their dogs momentarily having lost interest in one another.

"I've seen you here before," the woman went on. "Several times. I live across the street."

"Me, too. In 1440."

"I'm in 1510." She smiled as if that made them old and great friends. "I usually stop over there"—she indicated a refreshment kiosk beside the pond—"for a cup of tea. It's so nice and quiet this time of day. Before the schools let out."

"True," he said, gazing fondly at Shazam and feeling a father's pride.

"You are so beautiful," the woman cooed at the Afghan. "Look at how her coat shines. You must brush her a lot."

"Of course." It was one of his great pleasures.

They were passing the kiosk when the woman opened her purse.

"Would you do me a favor?" she asked, removing a small cup. "Would you be kind enough to go in there"—she indicated the men's room on the side of the building—"and fill this with water for Trixie? I'd go into the ladies' and do it, but I don't like it in there."

She looked up into his face with as pleading and sorrowful an expression as he had ever seen.

"I'll hold the dogs. Please?"

He couldn't deny the sad little woman so small a favor.

They exchanged Afghan for cup, and he went into the men's room.

He was filling the cup from a tiresomely slow faucet when he heard someone enter behind him. As he turned, before he fully recognized that it was she, a surgical scalpel sliced neatly through his jugular vein. She stepped back in time to avoid being splashed. She quickly wrapped the scalpel in a towel from the hospital at which she was head of the department of internal medicine, and left.

8

"Yes he can yes he can yes he can!" The boy, about seven, was screaming into the face of the black woman who had brought him to the playground. Hal couldn't hear her words of appeasement, but they clearly didn't work. The child turned his back on her and marched, like a grim little soldier, to the monkey bars. The woman, looking to heaven and saying a few words meant for her ears and God's only, went back to her bench and her knitting.

Hal glanced at his watch. Woodward was now half an hour late. He briefly went over his rehearsed explanation and thought he might try it again but decided not to, for the words, still echoing in his ears, sounded crazed.

He turned his attention to a breathtaking little girl who was being hoisted up ever so slowly on a seesaw by her mother. The woman was clearly slave to the child; her nonstop patter, meant to instill confidence at being so high off the ground, merely filled the child with recognition of the danger, and her enormous eyes were wide with fear. Hal wondered if Audrey had been treated like that child; if she had been the pride and joy and victim of her own mother.

As if on cue, the little girl started to bawl, and the mother scooped her up in her arms and made it all the worse.

He glanced at his watch again. Thirty-six minutes late.

He wondered what kind of child Betty had been. The image of a messy, tousle-haired imp came to mind, one who answered back and had freshness honed to an art. He recalled with pleasure how, when she and Andy first arrived, Hal's every word had been gospel. He, the king of comedy; they, the supplicants at his feet, there to learn and adulate. It had lasted a week.

"It *is* a good joke," Betty had said. "You just don't get it." She stood before Hal's desk in his office like a child expecting discipline before the principal.

Andy's eyes had turned to Ping-Pong balls at his partner's mutiny.

"I get it, I just don't like it," Hal answered.

"It's a good joke," she mumbled under her breath.

"Are you going to pout?"

"Yes." And the sight of that grown woman staring at the floor with a child's look of resentment on her face had so charmed him that he started to laugh.

"If you don't stop that I'm going to shave your head," he had said, and that made *her* laugh.

From then on, all was lost. Student became cohort, cohort friend, friend . . . ? What was Betty? he wondered. Best friend, he supposed. Partner in the crime of stolen jokes, old routines, rim shots. Comforter when the pain hit, cohysteric when it went away.

Funny, but he could no longer imagine life without her. Or Andy, of course, he added out of embarrassment.

Woodward was now forty-five minutes late. Hal walked to Fifth Avenue, found a phone booth, and called his number. No answer. He would call later, from the studio.

Run-through had already started when Hal arrived. He slid into a seat next to Betty in the darkened theater.

"How's it going?" he asked.

"The first scene lasts an hour and a half, even though Stu's got them talking like John Machita. Where were you?"

"Believe it or not, I was meeting somebody on the list."

"Somebody *live* on the list?"

"Yeah."

"Well? What happened? Give!"

"Shh!" the diminutive set designer and even smaller decorator hissed in unison from two rows behind them, like little snakes.

Hal took Betty by the hand, leaned forward a row to Andy, who was sitting beside Arthur the boom man, and said, "Take notes. Arthur, don't distract him." Then he hurried up the aisle, Betty behind him, to the small office they used during tapings.

There was one chocolate bar left over on the coffee table, and they split it.

"So?" Betty asked.

Hal produced the photocopy of the list from his pocket and indicated Woodward's name. "Him. He never showed. I guess he thought I was a nut."

"What did you say to him?"

"Nothing. I didn't have a chance. I was going to tell him when I met him."

"Tell him *what?* You know, Hal, in all of this, we still don't know what's real and what's your very fertile fiction writer's imagination." She wiped a chocolate smear from his lip.

"Old I am, senile I'm not." He took her hand from his mouth and kissed it.

There was an instant implosion, a short-circuiting between them. She stared at him.

"What'd you do that for?" she dared to ask.

"I don't know. Can't a friend kiss your hand?"

"Sure. A friend can kiss any part of me he wants to."

As soon as the words were out, she regretted them. And this time, her embarrassment couldn't be hidden. Her face, burning and reddened, was still raised to his.

He kissed her, for he felt she had asked it of him, and because to refuse would humiliate her further.

As his lips left hers, she burst into action.

"All right, that guy didn't show up. Let's call the next one."

"Let's? Is that short for 'let *us*'?" Hal asked.

"Until this thing is settled, you're no use to the show, and I'm not good enough yet to write it by myself so I better help you."

"Hey, did you just admit you don't know everything there is to know about comedy?"

"I said I'm not good enough *yet*. 'Yet' being the operative word here." She took the list from him. "All right, who are we up to?"

He glanced at the list over her shoulder. "That one. Ernst Goodman."

"Okay, Ernst." She crossed to the phone on the desk and dialed 411.

"What're you going to say?" Hal sat down and put his hands behind his head. It was wonderful to have an ally, and even more wonderful to be succored.

"Do I know?" she intoned.

"Are you Jewish?" he parroted.

"Is this information?" she said into the phone. "I'd like the number of Ernst Goodman at 15 East 68th Street. . . . Residence, I think. . . ."

"Not listed," Hal mumbled to himself.

"Yeah, thanks." Betty scribbled the number on the cover of the previous week's script. "All right, who calls?"

"I thought you were taking over here."

"I got cold feet."

"Call."

"What do I say?"

"What I've been saying."

"That gibberish?"

"Shut up and dial."

She did, and at the third unanswered ring was about to hang up with great relief when a woman's voice answered. After a small language problem was resolved, the woman being the Goodmans' Hispanic maid, Betty scribbled another number on the script and, thanking her, hung up.

"He's at *business*," she said.

"Then call him at business."

"I already made one call. It's your turn."

"Call, or from now on you take all the writers' meetings with the network."

Her fingers flew to the phone and she punched in the numbers. In a moment, Hal heard her ask for Ernst Goodman.

"He must be a lawyer," she said, her hand over the mouthpiece. "It's Goldstein, Goodman, Epstein, and O'Hara."

"What's O'Hara doing there?"

"Trying to get a word in edgeways."

Hal laughed. "And you say you're not antisemitic."

"I couldn't resist."

A woman's voice came on and said with great authority: "Mr. Goodman's office. Miss Breen speaking."

"I'd like to speak to Mr. Goodman."

"I'm sorry. Mr. Goodman is in conference."

"Could you tell me when he'll be free so I can call back? It's important."

"That won't be possible. After this conference, he has a conference call and a partners' meeting in the conference room, and then he'll be leaving the office for an outside conference."

"He goes to a lot of conferences, doesn't he?"

"May I have your name?" Miss Breen asked, obviously not amused.

"Elizabeth Lancing," Betty answered, totally cowed.

"And what is this in reference to?"

A twinkle came into Betty's eyes. "Uh . . . actually, I live in the apartment under Mr. Goodman, and there's water pouring down from my bathroom ceiling. . . ."

"Just a moment, please." Miss Breen put her on hold.

"Aren't you wonderful." Hal beamed at her.

"I learned from a master." She bowed her head in his direction.

"Hello?" A man's voice on the phone this time.

"Is this Ernst Goodman?"

"Yes. You say there's a problem at my apartment?"

"Not really, Mr. Goodman. I just said that so your secretary would let me talk to you. You see, your name is on a list and— "

"What? What are you talking about?"

"I'm trying to explain. There's a list, and three of the men on the top of the list are dead, and your name is—"

"I don't know what you think you're doing, but I don't have time for this kind of joke." And he hung up, but not before Betty heard him say in a tight, angry voice, "Miss Breen, in future . . ."

Betty turned to Hal and shrugged. "He wouldn't talk to me. I'm sorry."

"Hey, I couldn't have done any better. I liked the bit about the water."

"Thank you."

"Buy you a beer?"

"We're supposed to be in a run-through."

"Why?"

"To see if the script needs work."

"Why?"

"So the episode can be wonderful."

"Why?"

"So all the little kids who watch the show and all their mothers will laugh uproariously and keep our ratings up."

"Why?"

"So we can keep getting paid."

"Why?"

"So we can buy things we want. Like beer. Let's go." She gave up.

Hal became aware that he was staring at Betty's face, even making an unconscious assessment of it. The jawline, too plump; the eyes, speckled nicely but too round, so that she frequently appeared to be staring when she wasn't; the nose, too bulbous at the end; the mouth, full and well shaped, but the lipstick was always chewed off. All in all, a nice, ordinary face.

Why did it give him so much pleasure to be sitting there, staring at all those mistakes put together?

Because they were Betty, and Betty was . . . his friend.

"You want another beer?" he asked.

"I've had two already. Yes."

He signaled the waiter, who pointed at the hot hors d'oeuvres tray that had just been set up. Hal nodded. The bar was next to Studio 104, and the bartender and waiters knew the entire staff of *Family Business,* what they drank, who they drank with, who they bitched about, and how many drinks they could have before they chased away the other regulars. Perhaps it was Hal's signaling for another gin and tonic for himself that made the waiter recommend food.

"How long have you worked here, Chuck?" Hal asked him as he put down a plate of chicken wings, meatballs, and mystery meat pies.

"I started four comedies, two cop shows, and the early news ago. How come you guys are here so early?"

"We're playing hooky."

"Good for you." He leaned in to Betty. "You better watch this guy."

As he left, Hal remembered kissing Betty in the office at her unspoken suggestion. What was all that about? Friendship.

He realized he had never had a true and deep friendship with a woman before, and he told her so. He couldn't read the expression on her face when she responded.

"Yeah, I remember. You weren't raised to think of me as someone to talk to. You were raised to think of me as someone to fuck."

"Oh, Jesus, did I say that?"

"Unless there was some other male chauvinist mo-ron walking with us."

"Do you forgive me?"

"Can I leave in the cannonball joke?"

"No."

"Then I don't forgive you."

"Yes, you do."

"No, I don't."

"Yes, you do!" And he reached across the table and tickled her hard.

She squealed, too loudly. Several men at the bar who were watching *Live at Five* looked over, and the bartender turned up the volume."

"First you insult me, then you humiliate me," Betty said, staring into her beer. "Why do I love you?"

"I love you, too," he replied, but she didn't look up.

The next voice either heard was that of Sue Simmons on the news.

"The body of New York developer Simon Woodward was found hours ago in Central Park. . . ."

The stunned expression on Hal's face told Betty where she'd heard the name before.

". . . He had his throat slit. Outside the snack bar, his dog had been tied to a railing. Police are investigating the possibility of . . ."

"Are you all right?" Betty took Hal's hand in hers.

"He was on his way to meet me!"

"God, Hal!" And suddenly she fully understood what he had known for some time. *Men were being murdered*. "We have to go to the police."

"Yeah. Only first," he said as he slid out of the booth, dropping some money on the table, "we've got to make Goodman listen to us."

When they got back to the office, Andy and his boom man were sitting side by side, chatting self-consciously. Arthur nearly leaped off the couch when they entered.

"Sorry, guys, we need the hall," Hal said, hurrying to the desk.

"Don't you want to know how the run-through went?"

"No. Please?" Hal indicated the door.

Andy glanced at Betty. "Betty stays, Andy goes *again?*"

"Look," Hal blurted, "we're having an affair. We each hired a different caterer. We've gotta fire one of them before she buys extra lox."

"You're having—" Andy beamed.

"He's kidding," Betty jumped in.

"Is he?"

"He does it for a living. Go!"

A resentful Andy and a confused Arthur gotten rid of, Hal dialed Goodman's home number.

"What makes you think he's going to listen to you any more than he listened to me?" Betty asked.

"Because he won't be listening to me."

"Why not?"

Ernst Goodman answered his phone. Hal held up his hand to silence Betty.

"Mr. Goodman? Ernst Goodman?" he began.

"Yes."

"This is Detective Inspector Gleason of the nineteenth precinct."

After a pause, "Yes?"

"Did you get a call from a young lady within the last few days about your name appearing on a list?"

"Yes, I did. This afternoon, at my office. Why?"

"I'd rather not say over the phone, sir. Will you be home for the next fifteen minutes?"

There was a pause before he answered. "I can see you in an hour, if you like. I'm in conference till then."

Hal heard a muffled exchange between Goodman and a woman, Goodman's hand having been placed over the receiver.

"Very well," Hal answered. "I'll see you in an hour."

He hung up and turned to Betty. "Done."

"You're amazing. Only one thing."

"What?"

"Aren't detective inspectors from Scotland Yard?"

"I don't know." He put his arm around her waist and led her out of the office. "And luckily, neither did he. Let's eat."

Bentley's made the best cheeseburgers in Manhattan, and Hal and Betty sat in a booth separated by two of their finest, as well as side dishes filled with french-fried onion rings, potato pancakes, and baked beans.

"What, no spaghetti?" Betty said, surveying the table.

"I eat when I'm upset." Hal dipped an onion ring into a pool of catsup on his plate.

"And what d'you do when you're happy?"

"Eat. You wouldn't understand, being a shiksa."

"Here comes *Fiddler on the Roof* again." She folded a potato pancake neatly in four, dipped it into the accompanying applesauce, and put the whole thing in her mouth.

"It's true. Something annoys you, you reach for a

root beer. It gets worse, you add shaved ice, maybe a stalk of celery. But if I'm upset, like if guys are dropping dead all around me, I need grease and salt. Grease and salt can fix anything."

"Except the lining of your arteries."

"Keep your nose out of my arteries, if you don't mind."

"It's for your own good."

"Yes, Ma." He chuckled. "Are you absolutely sure there's not one drop of Jewish blood in you, Elizabeth Anne Lancing?"

"Uh-uh. Lutheran mostly, with a little Catholic thrown in to make me appreciate guilt. Why? Would you like me better if I was Jewish?"

"I don't think I *could* like you better." But the truth was that he would. He knew that. Audrey had so turned him off gentiles that it almost didn't make sense for Betty to be one. It made her suspect. Another reason to resent Audrey. She had turned him into a bigot.

"You know," he said, reaching over and putting his fork into the baked beans, "you don't have to go with me. I can talk to him myself."

"I have no plans. Stop that." She smacked his hand. "Don't eat from a serving dish."

He put the forkful of beans quickly into his mouth, lest she force him to put them back. "How come?"

"Because it's not polite."

"No, idiot, how come you have no plans? How come some smart thirty-five-year-old hasn't snapped you up?"

"Perhaps I prefer smart fifty-year-olds." Her eyes

remained on the food in front of her. "Besides, statistically I'm a lost cause. I'm over thirty."

"Big deal. The jockey shorts I've got on are older than you."

After a moment of silence, Betty asked, still without looking up, "Were you serious about getting a divorce?"

"I think so."

"I'm sorry."

"Yeah, me, too."

She helped herself to a big forkful of baked beans, taken directly from the serving dish.

Ernst Goodman pressed the palm of his hand against his bedroom door; it was hotter to the touch than it had been only minutes before. He looked down at the wet towels he had wedged along the floor. No smoke was coming into the room.

For the third time in that many minutes, he congratulated himself on his calm, born of years of corporate warfare. He had defeated so many combatants, he would defeat this one as well. He was sure of it.

He crossed to the open window, past the phone with its cord cut, and shouted down to the street twelve stories below. The small group of people was still standing there looking up, but now there were a few more. A woman with a baby carriage. An elderly couple.

There was little to do but wait for the fire department to get there, but inactivity was not his style: he was dynamic, always on the move, buying, selling, stealing, a conglomerate rather than an individual.

He went back into the bathroom and filled the wastepaper basket with water once again. He doused the bedroom door; there was no sound of hissing as the cold water hit the hot door, only the crackling on the other side.

The Manet had been sent out for cleaning. That was fortunate. The Dubuffet watercolor was behind glass, which might protect it. The Francis Bacon drawings were doomed.

He recalled their first setting, in his office. The mangled, melting bodies they depicted had intimidated many of his colleagues, just as he knew they would. He forgot why they had made their way into his home where they could intimidate no one.

He thought of his wife, who had been at a spa for three days. She would hardly feel the loss of the drawings, the Manet being the sole work of art that she appreciated, presumably because she had heard of Manet. Try as he had over the seven years of their marriage, he could not penetrate the wall of her ignorance. But there were compensations. Other penetrations.

He crossed back to the window and looked down at the street. The crowd was larger now, about a dozen people. One actually waved to him. He waved back.

Calm was a way of life. Calm in the face of business calamities. Calm in the face of takeover bids and tax evasion charges and cheating wives and women who threatened to tell everything. Calm.

He turned back into the room, and for the first time saw the thickened color of the air, the small curls of smoke coming in around the sides of the door.

More water. Two baskets full.

But still the air thickened and grew viscous.

He wetted a facecloth and held it over his mouth.

Calm.

He stood by the window and looked not at the crowd, but at the sky and then the skyline. This was his city. He was one of the few who owned and manipulated and contorted it to his purpose. He had come far from that lower-middle-class neighborhood in Philadelphia, but he still had farther to go. He would travel the distance. Nothing could stop him.

Calm.

And then, in one bursting flash of red and yellow and black, to the sound of a huge exhalation, the door became an arch of fire and the air opalescent.

Even in this he was remarkable. He drew a chair up to the open window, stepped up on it, and judged the ledge outside.

Their cab turned onto 68th Street from Fifth Avenue, and Hal immediately saw the crowd held back by the police in front of number fifteen.

"God . . ." he gasped, already knowing what was ahead.

They paid the driver, who had to back out of the street, and hurried into the crowd. The fire engines hadn't yet arrived, and the man on the ledge of the twelfth-floor window stood up there motionless, looking down, not at the street but at himself. The smoke behind him curled upward out of the window, and he appeared to be praying.

"It's not . . ." Betty started, but couldn't bring

herself to say his name, although she and Hal were both certain it was Ernst Goodman.

"It's my neighbor, Mr. Goodman," a woman next to her said, mistaking her unfinished statement for a question.

Hal pulled Betty to him and tried to turn her face from the frozen man and the deep gray smoke, but she stared, transfixed.

Then the shattering scream of a siren, several sirens, close and coming closer.

And the explosion. The sphere of red flames that knocked the man off the ledge and into space.

Betty pressed her face into Hal's chest and Hal's own eyes shut against the sight, but not against the sound of Ernst Goodman's body hitting the cement sidewalk not twenty feet from them.

And at the corner of 68th Street and Fifth Avenue, a woman in a red coat that smelled faintly of splashed gasoline hurried away.

9

Six months before Ernst Goodman was hurled from the ledge outside his twelfth-floor apartment, before Woodward was slashed to death in Central Park, even before Friedman was run over behind the Met, Audrey sat in a tub of hot water and suddenly found herself crying. Hal would be home from the studio in less than an hour and would want his dinner. And it would be her job to cook it and serve it and sit with him while he ate it and listen to what the new girl on his staff had said and what Glenda had done and "What's for dessert" and "What's on TV tonight" and "In China they consider a belch a compliment."

Her tears mingled with the bathwater as she thought back to Timmy, who was the only man she'd ever loved and the only man she would ever love. He was still somewhere in Kansas, in one of those towns where no one ever went and nothing ever happened. Still working in the relentless sun, that beautiful golden body with the soft-platinum furry spots and the one dark spot that was the most beautiful of all.

And true to her word, she would never see him again.

She wept.

Her fat husband was laughing at the TV set, and she thought, How many TV shows will I watch before I die?

"Get it?" Hal turned to her.

"I understand it." Audrey sighed. "I just don't think it's funny."

"You're just prejudiced because I didn't write it." And he turned back to the set, pleased with himself and sure of her.

What would he say, she wondered, if he knew how unhappy she was in this world he loved so much; this apartment and this city and the loud people and the endless jokes? Probably what her father had said: "We were not put on this earth to be happy, but to do God's bidding."

Well, she wasn't doing that, either. She was child-less and would remain so. Only Timmy had the power to force her to bear a child, to please him, to repro-duce him. And she imagined herself sitting on a porch at midday, the sweat running down her back, and a child, sick with the Kansas heat, crying in her lap.

She left the room, silently cursing herself and her husband and Timmy and her father.

She went to the gym twice a week, not that she cared about exercise or her body, but because there was nothing else to do. It was the most expensive gym she could find, because spending Hal's money quickly was at least some form of revenge.

One morning she became aware of two women

staring at her. That wasn't unusual in itself; she was used to being admired, and there were women who wished to do more than admire, but these two stood together, staring and whispering. They made an amusing picture: one was tall and stunning with dark red hair, the other short and squat with fingers lit up with pavé diamonds.

Audrey left the Nautilus machine and wandered over to a table that was set with crystal goblets and sterling coolers filled with bottles of mineral water.

"Whew, I'm exhausted," said a woman just behind her, leaning forward. Audrey turned and saw it was the tall one. "I've seen you around before," she went on. "I'm Sheila Federstein . . ."

They chatted while they poured their drinks and sipped, and Audrey relaxed and found the woman charming and certainly no lesbian.

"I'd like you to meet a friend of mine." Sheila held up a finger to beckon to the chubby lady, who was across the room, sitting idly on a stationary bicycle. She started to climb off, with difficulty.

"Yes," Audrey said brazenly, "I saw you two talking about me before."

"You don't miss much, do you?" Sheila laughed. "We were deciding who to ask to lunch. We're desperately bored with each other."

The one with the diamonds was Rosemary Monroe, and one would hardly have expected to see her in any gym, much less Joan's Women, for she hated exercise and was apathetic about her appearance. Audrey supposed she came to be with her friend Sheila.

They went to a small French restaurant that was filled with fresh-cut roses and women, like themselves, with nothing to do. It took no time at all for their conversation to turn to their husbands.

"Harold's in leather," Sheila said over the rim of her glass of mineral water. "Don't confuse that with 'into leather,' which might be interesting. He makes cheap purses. Really tacky stuff."

"There's a lot of money in junk." Rosemary dipped a crust of bread into one of her snail shells to soak up the buttery juice.

"How can you eat that?" Sheila scowled at her. "You know what that does to your arteries?"

"Sidney's a partner in a real estate development company," Rosemary said, ignoring her. "They build malls and shopping centers in bad areas."

"Harold's got two outlets in her husband's malls. Small world, huh?"

"Is that how you two met?" Audrey picked at her caesar salad. "Through your husbands?"

"Oh, no," and Rosemary chuckled until Sheila shot her a meaningful glance.

"We met on Fire Island," Sheila said. "I was visiting my brother and"—her voice lowered imperceptibly —"his lover. They're gay and they've been together twelve years, but they cheat like crazy. It works for them. Listen, it works for everybody." She shrugged and pushed her half a grapefruit farther away.

"I was thinking of buying a beach house," Rosemary said. "We met when the real estate agent brought me to her brother's house. I thought she was a dyke at first. I really did." She laughed and sucked up more butter sauce. "You know, living with two queers."

"Gays," Sheila corrected her.

"Gays," Rosemary parroted. "But she wasn't and I wasn't and we were practically the only ones on the island that weekend who weren't, so we spent some time together. You want a snail?" She held one out to Sheila.

"Please." The latter dismissed it. "What about you?" she said, turning her attention to Audrey. "What does your husband do?"

As much as it offended her to be questioned about Hal as if he defined her, Audrey answered, not without pride, "He writes *Family Business.*"

"You mean, on TV?" Rosemary's eyes widened for the first time since she had been served the escargot.

"Yes."

"How *glamorous*," Sheila said. "How incredibly glamorous."

"Not really." Audrey played with a leaf of lettuce.

"Are you kidding? Try living with shoulder purses for a while."

"Did he write the episode where Glenda Carpenter gets locked up in a subway train all night?" Rosemary momentarily stopped eating.

"Yes." Audrey almost blushed.

"It was so funny. Even Sidney laughed, which is a compliment because he has no sense of humor. It's true. I live with somebody who has no sense of humor."

"I envy you," Audrey said simply.

Sheila and Rosemary exchanged surreptitious glances.

"What's he like?" Sheila asked, and both women

stopped eating and drinking and awaited Audrey's reply.

"Self-involved."

"Really?"

"Well, which of them isn't? Husbands, I mean. Show me a husband who pays any attention to his wife, and I'll show you a man who's been married for less than a month." Rosemary went back to her snails.

"In what way is he self-involved?" Sheila asked, reaching for her grapefruit, not out of desire for it but to satisfy a need to appear uninterested.

"We live jokes around our house. Jokes and ratings and dialogue that isn't said right. That's all we talk about. We either watch television or talk about it." Audrey was starting to open up.

And if they were pumping her for information, she didn't notice.

When she got home, Meg told Audrey that her mother had called. She let the noxious obligation to return the call hang over her head for several hours before she dialed the little town in Kansas.

"Where were you?" Her mother's twang was shriller than usual. "I been waitin' all afternoon."

"Sorry. I was out."

"Is it hot there?"

Audrey winced at the question. Am I to be spared nothing? she thought. First they would discuss the heat, whether it was dry heat or humid, and then how dangerous the air could be in a city, and why didn't she bring her husband out for a visit so they could show him the local sights, and finally, inevitably, her draining need for money.

"Could you let me have a little something?" The question that was hanging in the air finally landed.

As soon as she assured the woman that a check would be sent out, the conversation ground to its usual halt. Then, just before they parted, the woman said, "You remember that boy you used to go with? What was his name?"

"Timmy." Her mother knew damn well what his name was. She had screamed it at her often enough when she thought her daughter was giving away what ought to be paid for with two dollars for a marriage license.

"That's him. He's dead."

Audrey said nothing; she stared, held her breath, a gland was spitting something into her blood that immobilized her.

"Some kind of machine accident. Cut him up," her mother added, and then, abruptly, "Got to go. 'Bye. Don't forget the check."

Later, when she could move, Audrey went to her purse, withdrew her checkbook, and wrote her mother a check for ten cents. She put it in an envelope with a note that said, "Here's the little something you called me for," addressed and stamped it, and asked Meg to mail it on her way home.

Then she went into the bathroom, drew a hot bath, swallowed half a bottle of tranquilizers, climbed into the hot water, and waited to die.

If she hadn't had such a large lunch or so many drinks to wash it down, she probably would have; but as it happened, twenty minutes later she sat sobbing in a tub of hot water and vomit.

They went to lunch regularly, she, Sheila, and Rosemary, and in a few weeks their lunches were the high points of her life. She had never had close women friends before, never shared with them her inner feelings, never heard theirs.

And now, the things she heard!

Sheila's first husband (she called her present one "the replacement") was a degenerate and could only maintain his erection if there were two women in bed with him. At first appalled by this, Sheila had resigned herself good-naturedly; after all, he didn't ask the women to do anything with each other, and it was a relief to have someone to share the burden.

Rosemary's husband was the opposite. He didn't worry about maintaining his erection, for he seldom had one. In appetites other than sexual, however, he was a gourmand like his wife.

"What about yours?" Audrey was asked one afternoon. "What's he like in the sack?"

She actually had to stop and consider before answering. "Okay, I guess."

"You *guess?* Aren't you there?"

"I don't care much about sex anymore."

"Who does?" Sheila agreed.

"Me," Rosemary said, pouting.

"Did you see *Fatal Attraction?* I was on her side a hundred percent. Where do men get off . . ." Sheila started.

And so the talk went to men, and if any consciousness was raised, it was of the shared anger and resentment against those three men in particular who had married and disappointed them.

They occasionally fought about money, she and Hal, but she usually got her way. Not so the day he came home in a bad temper to find their bed strewn with her new clothes.

"I thought I was supposed to look like the wife of a head writer," she said when his tirade had petered out.

"Like his wife, not his widow."

"What does that mean?"

"It means I'm fifty years old. I can't keep up this pace forever just to keep you and Bergdorf's on good terms."

"Fine. I'll return them."

"Did you have to buy so many?"

"I said I'd return them."

"Audrey, I swear, I'm not trying to make you walk around in rags, but have a heart. There's a couple of thousand dollars lying on the bed—"

"I said I'd return them! What more do you want?!"

"I want to stop feeling like I just murdered a Girl Scout. Come on," and his voice took on the cajoling tone that she hated more than the accusatory one, "you have enough clothes for now, right?"

"Right."

"You'll get some more later, okay?"

"Okay."

"You think I'm being unfair?"

"For God's sake, Hal, what do you want? My blessing? I'll take the fucking clothes back!"

Most of all she hated him when he bloated with guilt; when she could manipulate him like a fool; when his insipidity made her see how ruinous leaving Timmy had been.

She'd see him in hell before she'd return a thing.

Sheila and Rosemary had a secret. Audrey was sure of it. Sometimes, if she went to the ladies' room during lunch, they were deep in conversation about it when she returned and changed the subject abruptly or just stopped talking. She had to remind herself that they were old friends, that she was a newcomer, to keep from becoming jealous.

An attractive man was staring at Audrey. Hal was up for a Writers Guild Award, and they were at the ceremony, sharing a table with Betty and Andy and an entourage of producers. It was the first time Audrey had met Betty, and despite the latter's attempts to be gracious to her boss's wife, Audrey took an instant dislike to her. She was plain, not by nature but by choice. One of those political statements that Audrey despised. Andy, on the other hand, was adorable, but of no use to her.

The man at the next table, however . . .

She glanced over at him, and their eyes met and lingered so long that he grew embarrassed and looked away. She dismissed him as a window-shopper and briefly listened to her husband, who was holding court, as usual, with those who worked under him and had to listen. She, however, did not have to.

"Excuse me." She left the table and went into the hotel lobby, where a bar had been set up. The bartender was young and cute but, she decided, gay. What was it with men these days? Couldn't they appreciate a good pussy?

Audrey wandered with her drink to a print of a Cezanne that was hanging nearby. She smiled a bittersweet smile, remembering a day decades before when she and a friend, Sue Ellen, had looked at the same Cezanne print in a book in a library in Kansas.

"I can paint better than that." Sue Ellen had turned up her nose.

"No, you can't. Nobody can. He was a great artist."

"No, he wasn't. I never even heard of him."

"They have pictures by him at the New York Museum of Modern Art. That's how good he is."

"Fuck New York."

"Sue Ellen!"

"I mean it, and I don't care who hears me. Everyone is all the time talking about New York. Well, I don't care anything about New York. I like it just fine here."

"I'm going to live in New York someday. Or Paris."

"Get that idea out of your head, Audrey Philpot. You're going to live right here like the rest of us and die right here, too."

"No, I'm not. I'm already dying here."

"God, if you sing 'Moon River,' I'll puke."

And so Sue Ellen had stayed and had four children in five years, and Audrey had gone and had neither child nor career nor any of the things she'd held over Sue Ellen's head. No, she reminded herself, I do have one thing. I have a rich husband. And she washed down the bitter taste of her thoughts with the rest of her drink.

She turned to get another and saw him, the window-shopper, standing by the bar, staring again. But this time he smiled, and when she looked back provocatively, the smile widened.

"You're here with your husband," he said, approaching her.

"That's right. And your wife?"

"Home. With the children."

"I see. Buy me another?" She handed him her empty glass. "Gin and tonic."

His name was Sid and he was one of another army of producers on a rival sitcom. They chatted about the business until Audrey could no longer restrain herself.

"I don't give a damn about TV," she said.

"What *do* you like?" His eyes looked directly into hers.

"Fucking."

It was the third time they had met, appropriately enough at the same hotel in which Hal had lost his Writers Guild Award. It was afternoon, as usual, and they were naked in bed, as usual.

"Call down for lunch," Audrey said, stretching and arching her back so that her breasts stood up to excite Sid.

"Can't. I've got to get back to work."

"What? Come on." She cupped his testicles in her hand. "A little lunch, a little sex . . ."

"We already had a little sex."

"Maybe you had a little. I had a lot." She moved her hand to his flaccid penis.

"Sorry, babe."

She lay there for a moment, holding him, letting the rejection sink in, and growing angry.

"What if I said your leaving this early really upsets me?"

"Then I'd say you'll have to be upset."

"What if I get so upset I don't want to see you anymore?"

"Then I'll see somebody else."

She withdrew her hand and rolled over, her back to him. "Your words are hard but your cock isn't, so why don't you just get the hell out of here?"

He never answered. The mattress shifted as his weight was lifted from it; there was a shuffling sound, the creaking of a chair, the rustling of fabric on skin, and, sooner than she expected, the sound of the door being opened and closed. And all the while, as she listened to her lover leave her, she lay there despising her husband.

For surely, if he was any kind of man at all, she wouldn't have had to be in that room with Sid in the first place.

"What a pig," Rosemary said when Audrey told them the story at lunch the next day. "Are you going to finish your potatoes?"

Audrey slid them onto her plate. "But he did have a great body."

"How big did you say his body was?" Sheila leaned in, almost leering.

"About eight inches."

They laughed like schoolgirls.

"Men, cucumbers, dildos, vibrators, what's the difference?" Rosemary dribbled a bit of scalloped potato on the tablecloth and ground it in with an index finger. "Face it. We'd be better off with mechanical devices. At least you can shut them off when you're through with them."

"Speaking of schmucks." Sheila leaned back and sighed. "Did I tell you what the replacement did last night?"

It helped Audrey enormously that her friends hated men as much as she did. And it was a wonderful basis for a friendship. She lifted her glass of wine and happily listened to Sheila's story.

Once again, their secret. At the gym this time, Audrey came upon them in the dressing room, huddled together, their faces flushed with excitement. She saw them exchange telling glances after she had joined them, and for a moment she felt as suspicious of these women as she always did of men.

She felt almost sorry for Hal.

His cousin Joel, with whom he had grown up, was dying of cancer. Every day after work Hal went to the hospital and sat with him, and then came home filled with pain.

"Two-thirds of my life is over," he said one evening as they sat in their usual places in front of the TV set, "and you know what?"

"What?"

"I'm not sure what it was all about."

Neither of them looked at the other, but stared at the two women on TV who were interviewing a third, a victim of incest and rape.

"Joel's daughter comes to see him once a week and she lives crosstown. She thinks she's doing him a favor . . ."

Maybe she is, Audrey thought, remembering her own father who'd had no use for her and her own miserable weeks at his deathbed.

The victim started to cry and the camera moved in for a close-up.

"Sometimes I think I ought to retire and get a little house in the country. Just the two of us."

And go back to what I came from, the long, hot days of despair, she thought.

"We could have a garden . . ." he went on.

She'd had one. Hollyhocks and red poppies and shasta daisies. It had withered in the drought. Her mother had withered, too. Her skin looked like the change purses they sold in town in the five-and-dime.

"Would you like that?" Hal asked.

"If you would." Rubbish. He liked the way they lived, and whether she liked it or not made no difference, so why did he ask her?

The victim on television as opposed to the victim watching it, regained her composure and said that she regularly saw the relative who'd raped her at family affairs and that she never said anything to him.

"Maybe we need a vacation." Hal pressed the remote control, and they were staring at a herd of wildebeests stampeding across a river. "What about Mexico?"

"If you like."

A wildebeest emerging from the water near exhaustion was suddenly attacked by a female lion, which swiftly wrestled it to the ground. Its eyes were white and swollen with fear.

"Or Europe. We haven't been to Paris in a long time."

"Fine."

The lioness disemboweled the wildebeest with merciful speed, and her face came away red.

"A week in London. . . . Maybe we'll drive over to Bath. You liked it there . . ." Hal went on.

They'd been in Bath two years before. She was alone on a house tour in the Crescent when another Sid had started to look at her and she started to look back. He was a decade younger than she, in his early thirties, scruffy-looking and sensationally sexy. He wore faded old jeans, nearly worn out at the knees and rubbed almost colorless across the crotch. He had on a light sweater and nothing beneath, so that his nipples pushed outward on the yarn, and those two convexities plus the third, most intimate one held her in a breathless fever. He knew, for he smiled a small, tight smile and let his eyes slowly move over her body. They went from room to room that way, she breathless and dry-mouthed, he filled with juicy anticipation, until the tour was nearly over, and then, nodding toward a door marked W.C., he stepped inside, leaving it ajar. And if her breath had been difficult before, it was impossible then. The guide was leading the group toward the last of the public rooms when she held back and swiftly went through the door. The bathroom was small, designed for one person. She sat and he stood in front of her, and when it was done he stroked her cheek and said, "Thanks, luv."

As Audrey came out of her reverie, she realized she was watching two zebras fornicate and Hal was sleeping in the chair beside her.

Audrey hadn't had a cigarette in more than a year. Then one afternoon, standing there in the gym, glistening with hard-earned sweat, she had to have one. She turned to Sheila, who smoked, and asked for it.

"In my locker in my purse," Sheila panted, earning her own dew.

Audrey took the lapis-clasped purse down from the locker shelf, opened it, and found a pack of Marlboros. Putting one between her lips, she felt the familiar sweet stick and recalled someone saying, "One puff too many, a thousand cartons not enough." She hesitated for a moment, unsure of whether to take the risk, and then, finding a gold Dunhill lighter in the purse, lit up. That first puff took her by surprise; the heat of it, and the uncleanness. And then the dizziness. She stubbed the cigarette out on the concrete floor and felt the sensation of having been at the edge of a precipice and stepping back just in time. She opened the purse to drop the lighter and the cigarettes in, and saw a piece of paper.

There was no real reason for her to unfold and read it, but she did so without thinking.

Jason Rafferty, 1012 Fifth Avenue, NYC
Charles Landley, 169 East 78th Street, NYC
Fred Goldstein, 14 Central Park West, NYC
Dalton Phillips, 1421 Park Avenue, NYC
Samuel Friedman, Central Park South, NYC
Mervin Johanssen, 5 East 62nd Street, NYC

The name Samuel Friedman was outlined in red several times.

Her first reaction was to laugh. She was well aware that Sheila had a few casual encounters with men, but to make a list of those conquests was a male, not a female conceit. And then she thought, Why not? She quite liked the idea of women putting notches on their guns and carrying little black books. Brava the new equality. And the bastards still had to pay the bills.

She had barely refolded the paper and dropped it back into the purse when she turned and saw Sheila hurrying toward her, wiping herself with a towel. The sweat seemed only half from exercise; half, Audrey sensed, was from *fear*.

"Did you get your cigarette?" Sheila asked, taking her purse.

"One puff was as far as I got." Audrey indicated the crushed butt on the floor. "I forgot how they hurt."

"You're lucky." Sheila put the purse back in her

locker and spun the combination lock. "This way you won't start again."

Sheila always left her locker open, they all did; but now she carefully pulled on the handle to check that it was locked.

Because of a list of men with whom she had been to bed?

They went back into the gym together, and she was conscious of Sheila studying her as if for any reaction that was out of the norm.

So she slept around. Who didn't?

Hal had invited his writers to dinner, and Audrey was stuck with it. After showing them around the apartment and listening to their squeals about the size of it, she excused herself and hid in the kitchen while Hal entertained them.

Andy was definitely adorable. Too bad. Her feelings about Betty remained unchanged also. There was something about her that disturbed Audrey, something secretive in her attitude. If she was having a thing with Hal, that would explain it.

But that was ridiculous.

Audrey returned to the table and endured the three comedy writers' *witty* repartee. They discussed the executive producer ("the gonif"); the director ("one of the Philadelphia branch of the Hitlers"); the cameramen ("Larry, Curly, and Moe"); Glenda ("Queen of the Pig People"); run-throughs for the network execs (*"Invasion of the Body-Snatchers"*); the propman (*"The Creature from the Black Lagoon"*); the old Western star who'd guested on three shows ("The Cowboy

Store Druggie''); and on and on until she thought her head would burst like an overripe melon or her jaw would go into seizure from forced smiling.

"When I look at you two, you know what makes me happy?" Hal smiled lovingly at his writers, and Audrey closed her eyes against the sanctimoniousness of it.

"What?" Andy smiled back, preparing for praise.

"That someday you'll have writers who argue with you as much as you do with me. That's a head writer's prayer."

Betty laughed. "I don't argue. I express my opinion several times in escalating volume, that's all."

"How come I always get blamed for what she does?" Andy's smile faded into a comical little-boy pout.

"Because she's your partner. And besides, you always send her in to do the dirty work so you can be the nice one."

Andy hooted. "I didn't think you knew."

"I can always tell when Betty's bitching for herself or for you." Hal poured more wine into their glasses, ignoring Audrey's.

"Speaking of which," Betty said, "when can I use the cannonball joke in a script?"

"The day after we're canceled."

"We can't get canceled," she said hurriedly. "I'm buying a car."

"What d'you need a car for?"

"I thought I would drive it."

"In *New York?*" Hal grimaced.

"To get out of New York. You know, weekends in the country."

"Country? Which country?"

"Czechoslovakia."

"Oh, then you'll need a car."

"Audrey, how do you live with this man?" Betty asked, trying to draw her into the conversation.

Audrey knew the answer had better be *witty*, but instead she opted for using this clearing in the conversation to escape. "If you'll all excuse me, I've got the beginnings of a headache. I'll lie down for a while and leave you to your cleverness."

Betty's face looked positively stricken, which made Audrey's exit all the sweeter.

Later, Hal entered the bedroom.

"They're gone," he said, and she could tell from his tone they were going to have one of their fights. "Answer me something, will you?"

"What?"

"Have you noticed we don't have any friends?"

"We have friends," she said, running her thumb over her fingernails and studying her cuticles.

"No, we don't. Have you ever wondered why?"

She sighed. "How could I wonder why we don't have friends when I think we do?"

"Would you care to name them?"

Of all of Hal's tones of indignation, she thought she hated his sarcasm the most.

"No, I wouldn't care to name them."

"Because there aren't any."

"The McFaddens are our friends," she answered between clenched teeth.

"Then why do you call them the McFaddens instead of Elsie and Joe? Because they're not our friends. We see them a couple of times a year, if that."

"What do you want them to do, move in?"

"Everybody we meet is either not good enough for you or not smart enough or not rich enough . . ." His voice darkened. "Who do you think you are? Podunk royalty?"

She got up from the bed and headed for the bathroom and the other side of the door that locked.

"I brought home two dynamite people tonight. People who could enrich our lives and help us learn how to have fun again—"

"Help *you* learn!" She stood in the bathroom doorway, almost safe from him. "You! You're the one they talk to, not me! And they talk about things I don't know about! They were here to have dinner with *you* and you were here to have dinner with *them* and I was just the maid who served it!"

The slamming of the door echoed in the small bathroom with its hard tile surfaces. Then, when it was silent again, she heard Hal at the door.

"Audrey? . . . Look, I'm sorry you felt that way. . . . Come out and let's talk."

She turned on the bathwater and drowned his voice, wishing she could drown the rest of him as easily.

"Do you mean it?" Sheila asked, looking up from her Caesar salad. They were at their accustomed table in their accustomed restaurant.

"Do I mean what?"

"That you'd rather be a widow than a wife."

Audrey thought for a moment. "Yes."

"In that case—" Sheila started, but Rosemary cut her off quickly.

"We all feel that way sometimes. *It doesn't mean a thing.*" The intensity of her look to Sheila made the latter pick up her fork and resume eating without a word.

Audrey looked from one to the other. What on earth was going on?

"Is something the matter?" she asked.

"Why? Should there be?" It was clear that Rosemary would do the talking for both of them.

"Why are you two acting like that?"

"Like what?"

"You know like what. Like you have a secret and I'm not allowed to know."

"Honey, we don't have any secret."

"I think you do."

"Well, I can't help what you think. Can we change the subject, please?"

"Rosemary—" This from Sheila.

"I mean it," she said, cutting her off again. "Let's change the subject."

Audrey recognized the look on Rosemary's face: the forced calm and lying matter-of-factness. She had seen it on Sheila's face the day she saw the list. *The list. What was the list?*

"Does this have anything to do with that list of men in your purse?" she asked, turning to Sheila.

She required no answer. Sheila's face went white, and Rosemary, who always shoveled food into her mouth without stopping, stopped.

It took almost a minute of terrified silence before anyone spoke.

"Audrey, I'm going to trust you more than I've ever trusted anyone in my life," Sheila started, and Rosemary reluctantly nodded for her to go on.

"You can," Audrey replied, a little frightened herself.

"Have you ever joined a chain letter?"

"You mean one of those things where you send a dollar to the person on top of the list and add your name to the bottom?"

"That's right. So eventually when your name gets to the top, you get dollars from a lot of people."

"What about it?"

"There are different kinds of chain letters. Some are for money, some are for recipes, jokes, even . . ."

"Even what?"

Sheila stared at her plate, unable to continue.

"Even murder." It was Rosemary who found the courage to say it. "Murder the man at the top of the list and add your husband's name to the bottom. Then, when his name rises to the top, other women who have joined the letter will converge on him. One of them is bound to make you the widow you want to be."

It was a very long time before Audrey was able to say anything at all.

10

Hal sat in a small room at the police station. An overhead fluorescent light bathed the already grim room in gray, lest anyone miss the dourness of his surroundings. He felt as if he himself had committed all the killings and that he had come there not as a concerned innocent, but as a repentant murderer. His discomfort was caused by the officer whom he had told about the list and the deaths of Woodward and Goodman. A black woman, she'd stared at him with enormous brown eyes that seemed to take in everything and believe nothing. When she left the room, presumably to find another officer to whom he would have to repeat the whole story, Hal was filled with regret at having come to the police at all. But what else could he do? It was obvious now that every man on the list would die. It was also obvious that a fifty-year-old comedy writer who overate when he was upset was not the best-equipped person to save them.

The first officer, who was called Brice, returned with a surprisingly handsome young man whom she curtly introduced as Sergeant Winitsky. He asked Hal politely and in a deep voice of practiced resonance and authority what the matter was.

And all the while, as Hal went over the deaths of Phillips from electrocution and Friedman from a hit-and-run driver and Johanssen who fell off his terrace and Woodward who was attacked in Central Park and Goodman who was crushed next to him, Winitsky listened politely, but it was clear to Hal, who had spent thirty years among actors, that the man was merely acting.

After Hal left the police station, Brice followed Sergeant Winitsky to his office. He put the list Hal had given him and the three pages of notes he'd taken into a stapler and smacked down on the top of it. Then he added the stapled papers to the bottom of the highest pile on his desk. Seeing Brice's questioning expression, he said, "What's the matter? You never interviewed a nut before?"

"He didn't believe a word I said."

Hal sat at a tiny table in Betty's undersized kitchen. She sat on the only other chair, pushed into the corner. In front of them were mugs of coffee and a plate of Oreos.

"You notice we're always eating?" he added.

"How could he not believe you? You showed him the list. He could find out that all those men were dead—"

"Exactly. So could I. All I'd have to do is read the papers or watch TV, then type the names on a list, add a few I found in the phone book, and presto.

Another lunatic who gets his kicks from bothering the police.''

"He said that?!"

"No, but he thought it."

"But isn't he going to do anything?"

"Oh, sure. He's going to *look into it thoroughly*. That's what he said. I'll bet you all my rerun royalties that the list is in his wastepaper basket right now."

"I should have gone with you," Betty said.

"Why? So he'd think there are two imbeciles walking the city instead of one?"

"What're you going to do?"

"Right now? Right now I'm going to eat my Oreos, cream filling first, and then I'm going to figure out what else to do. Incidentally, you eat shit. That was not a directive. It was a comment on the food you buy."

"I like shit."

"So do I, but my malevolent better half won't have it in the house."

"So when you want shit, come visit me."

She said it lightly. Just a joke, nothing more; but there was more to it, and for the first time Hal recognized that Betty wanted him. It embarrassed him, for he had never thought of her in that way. Or had he? At what point does loving someone as your friend, your confidant, your partner in laughter and sadness, become loving someone as your lover? If sex was added to all the things that were already between them, would it really make a difference?

He put his hand over hers. "To coin a phrase, what would I do without you?"

"I'll bet you say that to all the shiksas."

"Actually, I don't. Not even to the ones I marry."

"Speaking of your blissful state, what're you going to do about Audrey? Are you going home to her tonight, knowing what you know, or are you staying here, with me?" Her face burned and it took all her nerve, but she was beyond making jokes that only hinted at what she wanted and how she felt.

"I'm going home to her."

Betty nodded and lifted her mug to her lips to hide behind.

"I have to. First of all, I gave that cop the list. I've got to copy it again—"

"What?!" Hot coffee dribbled out of the corner of her mouth. She didn't bother to wipe it away. "You're not going to continue with this thing! People are getting killed out there!"

"And the police aren't doing a damn thing, so I have to."

"Hal, for Christ's sake—"

"And I still don't know what Audrey has to do with it."

"The hell with what she has to do with it. Hal, please, you don't know what you're doing. You're not a policeman. You could get yourself killed. Hire a detective, if you want to, but keep out of it yourself!"

Her face was contorted with worry. He touched her cheek, and she kissed his hand. He said gently, "Now isn't the right time to—"

"Believe me, I know now isn't the right time. Just stay out of it, will you?"

"I can't. Not yet. Don't worry." He kissed her gently on the lips.

"Easy for you to say. I thought smart men weren't supposed to go in for that macho shit."

"You thought wrong."

It was after midnight when Hal got home. He had been away only twelve hours, but those hours had been so packed with drama and emotion that he felt them as weeks. Even the apartment seemed altered, smaller and sterile.

Could twelve hours change one's perceptions, or was he already estranging himself from home and wife?

There was a meal set out on the dining room table: slices of cold roast beef, tomato and cheese salad, and coleslaw under a sheet of plastic wrap, neatly arranged on a linen placemat with sterling fork and knife, cut glass goblet, and matching linen napkin. All the accoutrements of his empty life.

And he thought of junk food served up on a plastic table in the corner of Betty's impossibly small kitchen. And the warmth there. And the laughter.

Could he love the funny girl who seemed to love him? Could he walk into rooms with her on his arm without missing the envious looks on other men's faces that Audrey always brought?

Could he become at this late date a mensch?

He walked slowly to the bedroom, unwilling to face what might be waiting for him.

Nothing was waiting for him. Except a note on his pillow:

Hal,

I tried you at the office but they couldn't locate you. My mother was taken ill. It may be a stroke. I'm flying out. I'll call you in a day or two. Don't try to call me as no one will be at the house. Dinner's on the table.

Audrey

He had met Mrs. Philpot only twice in all the years of their marriage, and twice had been quite enough. She was a lean, angry woman with the face of a hawk and a preoccupation with her own laments: her parents had not permitted her to move to California when she was a girl, and all those golden opportunities had been lost; she'd married the first boy who asked her, to be out of her mother's house, and he'd died young and left no insurance; her only child chose to live halfway around the world. She did grudgingly admit that Audrey had married better than she had, but if that was intended to flatter him, it failed. It made his marriage sound like a business arrangement, which hit too close to home.

And now the old woman was dying, and the war between her and her daughter might come to an end. But that was no longer his business.

He went to the dresser and withdrew the list.

Harold Federstein, 1 East 87th Street, NYC.

He would go see Harold Federstein first thing in the morning.

No, of course that wouldn't do. He went to the phone and soon had the number. He started to dial, knowing that if Federstein would see him, he would have to meet him immediately, as exhausted and played out as he was.

"Hi, you've reached the home of Harold and Sheila Federstein," a man's voice announced, "who are out of town till Friday . . ."

He was mercifully given one more day before he had to convince this stranger that his life was in danger.

He lay down on the bed and continued to look at the list.

Malcolm Terrell, 124 Riverside Drive, NYC
Sidney Monroe, Glen Cove, L.I.
Frank Altshul, 12 Fairview Road, Greenwich, Ct.
Paul Davis, 117 West 86th Street, NYC
Todd Klemm . . .

And he was asleep.

11

The Red Finches Inn on Lake Waramaug was a page from a Connecticut calendar; the inn and its cabins clustered on the gentle slope of a hill that led down to the water. The lake, large and underdeveloped, lay in a valley surrounded by hills on which the estates of the mighty whispered their wealth. It was a perfect place to take Sheila for a little R and R, Harold thought.

Poor kid, she was all worn out. He didn't question what had worn her out, since his wife had neither job nor children nor charities to occupy her time. It was enough that his child/wife, his gorgeous auburn-haired baby doll, was cranky and needed a few days off. Off from what? Who cared?

He left the business to his nephew Sherman to run till Friday, ran the Jaguar through a car wash because you had to look good when you went new places, and packed his baby doll and three Armani sports jackets into the car.

The first day went beautifully, despite the presence of someone in another cabin who drove an XJS. Harold made a point of mentioning, when he and

Sheila met the man and his wife, that he preferred the styling of the XJ6, which was, to his way of thinking, a "classic."

The second day was also proving to be a delight (Sheila hinted that they would make love that night, for her nerves were calmer) when something unforeseen happened. He returned from a local antique store with the Victorian teapot Sheila'd sent him back for (she'd changed her mind about it being overpriced) and found her in their cabin on the phone, clutching her cheek.

". . . All right. . . . Look, it'll take me about an hour forty-five to get there. Tell him he's got to stay. It's an emergency. I'm dying."

She hung up and looked over at him in torment.

"Hey, toots, what's the matter?"

"My whole jaw fell apart."

"What?"

"Two of my inlays fell out. I'm in agony. I'm going in to Dr. Yarosh. Give me the keys to the car."

"Don't be foolish. I'll drive you."

"Harold," and baby doll's voice narrowed and became shrill, "don't argue with me. I want to drive myself. You stay here and have a good time. I'll be back in time for dinner."

"What am I going to do here without you?"

"You'll find something. I don't want to ruin your day as well as mine. Give me the keys."

"Toots—"

"Don't toots me, just give me the keys!"

And so she left him there in the parking lot, after mentioning to several of the staff that she was in agony and they should look after him until she got back that evening.

Harold decided to walk to the next inn around the lake for a late lunch. It served German food, and this was a perfect opportunity to indulge his love of wiener schnitzel without Sheila reminding him of his weight. He huffed his way down the lawn of the Red Finches, to the road, crossed to the lakeside, and headed north.

Two teenage boys passed him going the other way. They were blond, slender, and long-waisted, the kind of build he'd never had and never could have had, given his genes. No, he had fat Slavic genes, but his business had grossed eleven million the year before and those skinny blond kids would be lucky if they didn't pump gas for a living their whole lives.

He puffed along, now sorry that he'd decided to make the trek all the way around the lake for wiener schnitzel that probably was not that good anyway. He said a silent prayer that Sheila hadn't forgotten to release the emergency brake when she sped off, as she frequently did, and slowed his pace sufficiently for him to stop panting.

He was wrong about the wiener schnitzel. It was terrific. And the potatoes were dynamite. And the white chocolate mousse was out of this world. He missed his baby doll, but he had to admit to himself that it was a pleasure being alone to eat what he wanted without the lectures. A nice, well-rounded belch punctuated his thoughts.

And then he saw the blonde sitting by herself two tables away, looking at him.

She smiled and nodded.

He smiled back, but it was a smile and nothing more. When you had a beauty for a wife like he did, you didn't fool around. You didn't even kid around.

Unfortunately, the blonde didn't know this about him. She got up and came over.

"Hi," she said in what he supposed was her come-hither voice.

"Hi, yourself." He was loud and friendly and obviously not interested. "Have a seat. I was just about to have a cup of coffee. Would you like to join me?"

She said she would, but her voice was still low and sexy. Oh, well, he knew what to do next.

"My wife and I are staying around the lake." He noticed her wedding and engagement rings. Two carats, tops. Nothing to fall down over. "You and your husband staying here?"

"No, I'm here by myself."

"Oh. My wife had to rush to New York, but she'll be back. A couple of fillings fell out. I'd hate to tell you what her mouth cost so far."

The blonde smiled and lowered her eyelids. She was not getting the point.

"I wanted to drive her, but she wouldn't let me. She didn't want to ruin my afternoon. She should be back in an hour."

"That's nice. I was going to go for a canoe ride after lunch."

"Oh, yeah?"

"I rented one. It's down the road about a mile. But

to tell you the truth, I'm a little frightened to go by myself. I've never driven a canoe before.''

"I can tell. You don't drive it. You paddle it."

She laughed loud and long, and when she stopped her demeanor was different. She wasn't on the make anymore, or so it seemed to him. Just friendly and cheerful.

"You see why I'm frightened?"

"It's nothing. You put it in this side"—he mimed working the oar—"then you take it out and put it in this side . . ."

"You look like my husband at the discotheque. No, I'm not going. I'll return the canoe and stay on land where it's safe."

"Don't be foolish, it's nothing . . ."

And before he knew what he was doing, Harold had promised to take the friendly blonde for a canoe ride.

She sat there in the canoe, smiling out over the stunning lake, trailing her hand (the one with the two-carat diamond ring) in the water.

"I'll never be able to thank you for this," she told Harold, who was huffing and paddling, "but at least you'll permit my husband and me to take you and your wife to dinner tonight, all right?"

"It's no big deal," he protested.

"Please? He's getting here around six. You'll like him."

"Yeah? What does he do?"

"He's a caterer."

"Oh, yeah? Does he cook around the house?"

"He doesn't cook at all. He has two people who work for him who do."

Harold did some computations that added up to the opinion that the ring must have been bought on time, even though the blonde looked like she was made of money.

"Oh, look." She pointed at the shore, where half a dozen weeping willow trees stood lined up at the water's edge. Their combined branches made a tunnel parallel to the rocky shore. "Can we ride through? It looks so beautiful!"

"Sure, why not?" Harold paddled.

"Stop, all right?" she said when they were halfway through. "Let's just sit here for a minute. It's so peaceful."

He put the oar across the middle of the canoe, between them, and looked down into the shallow water.

"Look at the fish," he said. "I wonder if that's a trout, the big one. We should have brought a fishing pole with us. You know how long it's been since I went fishing? I think Eisenhower was president. I went deep-sea fishing off Montauk with a couple of—"

He never finished the sentence, for the brick the blonde had hidden in her purse caught him on the side of the head with such force that he was unconscious before he fell forward into the water.

She stood in the water up to her waist and held his face under until she was sure he was dead. Then she overturned the canoe on top of him and climbed out of the water quickly.

Her car was parked beside the road not fifty feet from where his body floated. It had been rented with false identification that had taken her the better part of two months to get.

She opened the back door, got a towel, and dried her legs. Then she changed her shoes and got in.

She drove away, around the lake, past the Red Finches to Route 202, and south toward the city.

In all her life, Audrey Philpot Grimes Newman Fisher had never felt so elated.

12

Hal tried Federstein's number for two days, but the machine was on and the message the same. He never spoke, for what he had to say was difficult enough to tell a person, impossible to tell a device.

He did, however, reach Malcolm Terrell, who told him that if Hal bothered him anymore, he would call the police.

Hal almost called them himself, but he knew that the handsome Sergeant Winitsky would laugh it off politely. Or perhaps he'd say, "Bother me anymore and I'll call Malcolm Terrell." The whole thing had its lunatic funny side. There he was, trying to help these men, even save their lives, and everybody wanted him to go away.

Maybe he ought to. Just forget the damn lists, leave Audrey, move in with Betty (Where did that come from? he wondered), write a decent episode instead of the crap he'd been doing recently, go on a diet, see his dentist twice a year, and just *live*.

But of course he couldn't. If you see an accident about to happen, you always yell *"Stop!"* even if it's in the library and everyone wants you to be quiet.

Audrey never called from Kansas, and when she did reach him at the office, she was already home. Mother Philpot had had neither stroke nor heart attack nor seizure. She'd had a bad clam roll. It served her right for eating seafood so far inland.

It was on the third day of waiting to speak to Federstein that Hal finally got through.

"Hello?" a child's voice answered his phone call.

"Hello, is Harold Federstein there?"

"This is Tanya," the little voice said.

"Hi, Tanya. Is Harold Federstein there?"

"Tanya Morris. Who's this?"

"This is Hal Fisher. I'd like to talk to Harold Federstein, okay?"

"Do I know you?"

"No, sweetheart. Is Mr. Federstein there?"

"You mean Uncle Harold?"

"That's right, darling. Would you tell Uncle Harold to come to the phone?"

"Everybody's here. Even Uncle Stanley."

"That's nice, dear. But—"

"We're eating now. I have to go."

"Wait a minute, Tanya, sweetheart. Look, tell Uncle Harold that a man called and he's coming over in about an hour. Can you remember that?"

"Yes, I can." Tanya sounded offended.

"Will you tell him?"

"I said I would, didn't I?" And she hung up.

The run-through was half over when Hal glanced at his watch and saw that it was after six.

"I've got to go," he told Betty and Andy, who

were arguing about a joke. "I'm going to see Federstein."

"You want me to come?" Betty asked, and Andy wondered, for the hundredth time, what the hell they were talking about.

"No, honey. You've done enough. Besides, somebody's got to run this piece of shit into the ground."

"Call me at home later?"

"Sure."

After Hal was out of earshot, Andy spoke.

" 'Somebody's got to run this'? What does that mean? Are you my boss now, too?"

"Don't be silly."

"I'm not being silly. I'm being a very well adjusted homosexual who is trying to avoid plunging into a paranoid fantasy. Look, I know you're in love with Hal and I know you two are doing it—"

"We're not doing it."

"All right, then, you're not doing it, but is that any reason for him to promote you over me?"

"He didn't promote me. He doesn't even know what he's saying. He's upset."

"About what?" he asked with an edge of belligerence. "I'm getting tired of being the only one around here who doesn't know what the hell is going on!"

"All right, I'll tell you. Just don't get hysterical."

"I never get hysterical."

"You always get hysterical."

"You want to see me get hysterical? Try not telling me for another ten seconds."

So Betty told him. And when she was finished, Andy was hysterical.

* * *

When Hal got to 1 East 87th Street and told the doorman he wanted the Federstein apartment, he was immediately told the number and to go directly up. So much for East Side security, he thought, but it was a relief not to have to fight his way past the building's watchdogs. Mingus would have been scandalized.

He stepped out of the elevator to find that there were only two apartments on the floor, which meant that Federstein's apartment was large and, like all the other men on the list, he was rich.

He rang the doorbell after noting that the Cezanne print on the hallway wall was not the mass-produced kind he'd had as a kid, but the genuine numbered and stamped article. He guessed that Federstein only kept oils inside the apartment.

A plump woman opened the door, and Hal heard others murmuring inside.

"Come in," she said, as if she'd expected to see him. "I'm Rosemary Monroe." She extended a hand toward him that had two pavé diamond rings on it.

"I'd like to see Harold Federstein," he said.

"Oh, he's not here." She smiled sympathetically. "Besides, the viewing was over yesterday. They buried him this morning."

Hal stared.

"My God, didn't you know?"

"No."

"I'm so sorry. The poor man was killed in a boating accident."

"When?"

"Two days ago. Why don't you come in? The family is sitting shiva. That's like a wake. I know

131

Sheila would be glad to see you. Can I get you something to eat?"

"No, I can't stay."

"You look white as a sheet. Are you sure you better not sit down for a minute?"

Hal glanced past her. There were about a dozen mourners standing about, eating, drinking, and speaking in hushed voices. All hushed except for Audrey's, which stood out.

He fled.

He walked across Central Park toward the West Side.

Audrey hadn't seen him. She was too busy consoling the widow. Or congratulating her.

Once more he was too late.

Another one murdered.

Another *husband*.

His mind was on high, trying to figure it out. He had the same awareness he had when reading a mystery novel or watching a whodunit. He sensed he had all the facts. Now he just had to manipulate them into a full understanding of what was going on.

Why was Audrey at Federstein's home?

Did all the wives of the slain men know each other? Did they all chip in to hire a killer for the group? Did they hold murderware parties, like Tupperware parties where they sold each other the latest in garrotes, guns, and poison?

Enough. He would get the list from the apartment and once again look into the respectful, full-of-shit face of Sergeant Winitsky.

He simply couldn't take any more.

*   *   *

Alone in their bedroom, Hal sat wearily on the bed and unfolded the list that lay in his lap.

Malcolm Terrell, 124 Riverside Drive, NYC.

He was too tired, or he would have shuddered at recognizing that Federstein's name, like the man himself, was missing.

Sidney Monroe, Glen Cove, L.I.

"Come in. I'm Rosemary Monroe." He recalled the fat woman with the rings from Federstein's apartment. Tired as he was, his mind started to grind. He *had* to understand this.

Frank Altshul, 12 Fairview Road, Greenwich, Ct.

Was there a Mrs. Altshul? And was she at the shiva, too?

Paul Davis, 117 West 86th Street, NYC.

Just crosstown from Federstein's apartment. Did that mean anything?

Todd Klemm, Trump Plaza, NYC

Rich, richer, richest.

Hal Fisher, 166 Central Park West, NYC.

He stared at his name like someone studying a forgotten mathematical symbol from his school days. Seeing them in that most unexpected of places, those words that meant him somehow meant nothing.

And then his mind unfroze and he ran out of the apartment.

"Hold me," he said when Betty, wakened from an early nap, finally opened the door.

She did, and for the first time in his life, Hal did not make love to a woman, they made love to each other.

There were moments when he gave himself up to her and she held him in her arms the way a man held a woman, and then suddenly it was changed around and he owned her, and nothing seemed wrong and nothing gave anything but pleasure and happiness and he was inside her and she was inside him and their mouths were one mouth and their bodies two halves of one starving animal feeding on itself.

When Hal awoke, it was ten o'clock in the evening. Betty sat across the room from the murphy bed in a wicker chair, reading one of a stack of unsolicited manuscripts for the show.

"Any good?" he asked, smiling at her.

"You or the script?"

"The script. I know I'm good."

"You're right. Unfortunately, this script is not. It's about Glenda getting scared by a neighborhood mugging so she takes karate lessons and becomes a public enemy. However"—she lifted the top script from the stack—"it's head and shoulders above this one, wherein Glenda's eleven-year-old nephew becomes a sleepwalker because a girl refused to go out with him, which is still eons better than this one"—she indicated another script—"wherein the entire family goes on a health kick and old Uncle Benjamin breaks out in a rash due to too much vitamin C and they think he has AIDS. Incidentally, I guess it's safe to say I love you now."

"Very safe." He held his arms out to her, and she hurried into them.

"What time is it?"

"Around ten."

"Why did you let me sleep?"

"I figured you needed it, after the workout I gave you."

"You want to know something?" He twirled a lock of her hair around his finger. "It's never been like that for me before."

"Really? Funny, it's always like that for me."

He yanked on the lock. "Tell the truth. I'm an old man. I need all the reassurance I can get."

She kissed the hand that held the lock of her hair, and he released it. Then she said, "I never made love with anyone I loved before. It's better."

He almost said, "Does that mean we're engaged?" but stopped himself. Even now he didn't know what he felt.

"Got any more Oreos, doughnuts, nacho chips or Spaghetti-O's? I didn't have dinner."

"You get real food," she said, bounding out of the bed, "now that you put out."

Betty's version of real food was frozen microwave lasagna and canned peas. As she heated them, she chattered away gaily.

"You know, just this afternoon Andy said we were doing it and I said we weren't . . ."

Suddenly, with a shock wave that resounded throughout his body, Hal remembered the list.

". . . I'll never convince him I was telling the truth. . . ."

The list with his name at the bottom.

". . . I still don't believe it is the truth. . . ."

The list of husbands whose names rose up until they fell off the top—

". . . I know I shouldn't be saying these things to you. . . ."

—as each of them died—

". . . It's certainly not cool. . . ."

—and disappeared from the list to be replaced by another husband added to the bottom—

". . . It's my turn for a little reassurance. . . ."

And instantly Hal understood everything.

". . . So? Any kind words would be greatly appreciated." Betty turned and saw his face. "What is it? What's the matter?!"

"The list."

"What about it?"

"I know what it is."

"What?"

"It's a chain letter."

"What are you talking about?"

"A chain letter of husbands. When you move to the top, you get murdered by the wives. Drowned or burned or run over or electrocuted or—"

"Hal, stop it! What on earth made you think of such a ghoulish thing?"

"Because Audrey put me on it."

13

Rosemary popped the cork on the bottle of Perrier Jouet, and Sheila and Audrey simultaneously held out their flutes. They were alone in Sheila's apartment.

"Me first. I'm the widow."

"Me first. I'm the reason you're the widow."

"She's right. Audrey first."

The living room was a mess, for Harold's side of the family believed in drowning their sorrows in food; there were half-empty plates everywhere, and someone had even had the nerve to put an uneaten pastrami sandwich into the piano.

"You know the first thing I'm going to do?" Sheila smiled over the edge of her glass. "I'm going to put this barn on the market and move into the Carlyle. I don't ever want to own anything again. Possessions possess you. I'm going to head east and keep going. London, Bruges, Florence . . ."

"Not me," Rosemary chirped. "When it's my turn, I'm going to buy everything in Manhattan from 59th Street to 72nd. I'm going to keep going until my charge card melts. What about you, Audrey?"

Audrey refilled her glass, feeling quite tipsy. They

were working on their second bottle since the mourners had left and the wake had become a celebration. Her first, unspoken answer was that she would return home in triumph and buy Timmy's freedom from whatever prison he had gotten himself into, whether it was a marriage or—

But, of course, Timmy was dead.

"I don't know," was all she could answer half-heartedly.

"Come on." Rosemary picked over a tray of hardening hors d'oeuvres. "There must be something you want."

"Just to be rid of him. That's all."

"That's the way I felt about Harold," Sheila said, reaching for the bottle, "but now . . . I don't know. He wasn't all bad. And he was nuts about me."

Rosemary laughed so they could see the mushrooms in her mouth. "You picked a fine time to change your mind. At his wake."

"Oh, I don't regret having him killed. It's just that . . . I'll miss him, too. You know, bittersweet."

"Not for me." Audrey took the bottle. "I'm going to love not ever hearing his whining again. Not ever having to sit there, the wife of the genius, and watch him play lord of the universe. God, you can't imagine the joy of not listening to another joke, of not saying 'Yes, dear, that's funny' when it's something he wrote and 'No, dear, that's not funny' when it's something he didn't write. And the thrill of not hearing about his sainted mother and his blessed father. And not having to look at that smug, pretty face of his ever again." She took a sip of champagne from the bottle.

"Is he pretty?" Rosemary cut away the dry rind of a half-eaten piece of Swiss cheese and popped the rest into her mouth. "Got a picture?"

"Sure."

Audrey rummaged around in her purse for her wallet. There was a picture of both of them, standing arm in arm with Warren Beatty. Unfortunately, Hal was in the middle, or she would have cut him out of it long ago.

"Here."

Sheila took the snapshot. "He's kind of cute—oh, my God! Is that Warren Beatty?!"

"Yeah. It was at an opening-night party. A friend of Hal's wrote the play."

"Gimme!" Rosemary grabbed the picture.

"You actually met Warren Beatty?!" Sheila shrieked.

Rosemary stared at Beatty.

"What was he like?" Sheila went on.

Rosemary's eyes moved to the man next to Beatty.

"Oh, shit," was all she said.

14

It was almost midnight when Hal and Betty arrived at the police station. They asked for Sergeant Winitsky at the desk, and a policeman with a purple stain on his cheek in the vague shape of a tree told them he was off duty. They asked to see someone else; he asked what for; Hal told him; he stared, openmouthed. Then, remembering that he was a policeman and above surprise, he disappeared through a doorway behind him.

"If I have to repeat this whole thing one more time," Hal groaned, "I'll go out of my mind."

He did not have to repeat it. A shirtsleeved man in the large central room of the station, which Betty was amused to find looked like the set of *Cagney and Lacey*, cut him off in mid-sentence.

"You said you already spoke to Sergeant Winitsky about this?" The man stretched his arms upward so that two circles of underarm perspiration were all one could focus on.

"Yes. A few days ago."

"Then it's his case. Why don't you come back in the morning and fill him in on it." His eyes darted across the room to something that presumably held more interest for him.

"You don't understand." Hal tried to modulate his voice, though he felt like screaming. "Somebody's trying to kill me!"

The policeman's eyebrows, full and bushy and gray, rose almost imperceptibly. "You've been threatened?"

"Not exactly, but my name's on a list—"

"Did you receive any kind of threat, either verbally or in writing?"

"No, but—"

"Was an attempt made on your life?"

"Not yet, but—"

"In other words, you *surmise* that someone wants to kill you?" And the sweaty man's eyes darted across the room again; he had lost interest.

"I'm fucking sure of it!"

Betty placed a calming hand on Hal's.

"Perhaps you shouldn't go home tonight," the man said, and the gentleness of his response was unexpected. "Then in the morning you can speak to Winitsky. Have you someplace to go?"

"He does," Betty answered, and the policeman's eyes focused across the room and stayed there.

They returned to Betty's apartment, tired, frightened, and, as was their custom, hungry.

"She doesn't have to kill me," Hal said as he read the ingredient list on the bag of sour-cream-and-chive potato chips. "All she has to do is wait until you do it for her. Listen, if I get out of this alive, I'm sending you to cooking school so we can quit eating chemicals."

"Some of my best friends are chemicals. You want a glass of cola-flavored carcinogens?"

"Who could resist?"

They ate their chips and drank their sodas in silence. And then Betty opened the top drawer of her dresser and removed a wrinkled, half-empty pack of Merits.

"Speaking of carcinogens." She held out the pack to him.

"No, thanks. I didn't know you smoked."

"Only when I'm terrified."

"Come here."

She did, and he held her until both of them stopped shivering.

15

Across town, another compulsive eater was pacing back and forth. Rosemary had the phone cradled against her neck, and when she wasn't speaking she was taking small bites of a hurriedly made corned-beef sandwich.

". . . That's right. . . . We haven't got a clue if he knows or not! . . . Why the hell else would he have come here? . . . Sheila doesn't know. . . ."

Audrey was pouring out the coffee they had made to help clear their minds.

". . . That's the only thing we can do. . . . Right. . . . To be on the safe side, Hal Fisher has got to go to the top of the list. . . ."

Audrey's hand started to tremble, and Sheila took the pot from her.

". . . Okay. . . . Yeah, I'll make some calls, too." She hung up and turned to Audrey.

"You'd better get home and pack."

"Why?"

"You know you're not supposed to be around when it happens."

"But it's not going to happen tonight—"

"Who knows when it's going to happen? They're putting all the wives on notice. Nobody else is touched until your husband is dead."

16

Hal lay cradled in Betty's arms, his cheek against the warm, damp recess just beneath her breast, and despite the comfort of that warmth, he started to cry softly.

"What is it?"

"Terrible."

"I know."

"No. It's terrible to love someone who wants you dead. Am I so loathsome—"

"Don't turn this on yourself. It's not you, it's her."

"No, it's me. It must be." And he wept.

She held him until the crying and the talking stopped and he was asleep.

17

Audrey stood in front of their apartment door, key in hand, afraid to go inside. She painstakingly went over everything that Rosemary had told her.

There was no real way of knowing whether Hal had seen her at the wake.

Nor did they have any proof whatsoever that he knew anything about the list. He could have had another reason for coming to Harold Federstein's apartment.

The one thing she must not do is panic. She must go inside, wake him, and say that her mother was ill again and the doctor had misdiagnosed her last attack. It was her heart. Then she must pack and go to the airport. She was to take the first available plane out of there and somehow end up in Kansas and stay there until they called her with the tragic news.

There was no way Hal could possibly know about the list.

No way at all.

She put the key in the lock and turned it.

Inside, the apartment was as she'd left it. The note she'd left Hal to tell him she'd be home late and to order in dinner without her was still on the hall table. All the lights were out. As she passed, she glanced into the dining room. There was no evidence that he'd had a meal there.

Her hand preceded her into the bedroom, felt around the wall for the switch, and turned the lights on.

He wasn't there.

Suddenly the panic was all around and inside her. It was after one in the morning and he wasn't there!

She ran to her dresser and pulled open the center top drawer. The jewelry box was sitting there, where it always was. She opened it without breathing.

The list was gone.

It took nearly an hour for Audrey, sitting in the first-class lounge at the airport, to notice the man who was staring at her. He sat across the room behind a copy of *Esquire* magazine and divided his attention between the two of them. He was approximately Hal's age but lean and natty and hawklike in appearance; the kind of man Audrey had come to expect to be as arrogant in bed as he was in business. She preferred it that way. For her, sex was an act of mutual conquering, not a mewling, saccharine act of love.

Audrey permitted the man to know that she was aware of him, this by looking at him, holding her defiant stare until their eyes met, and then glancing away. This would be repeated several times until they found themselves staring openly at each other. Then she would smile with a careful mixture of embarrassment and amusement and reel in her prey.

It was precisely the way she had engineered her first meeting with Hal years before.

They had been at the theater, she alone, he with a group of friends. He was thinner in those days and wore a jacket she recognized from a window at Bergdorf's. Standing at the bar, ordering a round of drinks for his companions, Hal had seemed self-assured and the kind who would pay for what he got, and that made him very right for Audrey. She was at that time and for weeks to follow unemployed, having been dismissed from a secretarial job through the pressure of her boss's wife, who was right, of course, but late, for Audrey had already received the fox jacket she wore that evening and the moonstone ring she twirled on her finger. I have a sixth sense about men, she reminded herself, assaying the stranger in the three-hundred-dollar jacket. And the Gucci shoes. And the gold watch. A Jew, to be sure, but a good-looking one. She liked Jews. They were rich and vain and generous if you happened to be blond and spoke like a lady. That she did, for every evidence of midwestern twang had been rooted out of her, as well as all traces of her barren beginnings. Being a woman was Audrey's career as well as her pleasure.

And she was very good at what she did.

At that moment what she did was to position herself in Hal's line of vision and wait for the inevitable to happen. It did, quickly. She stared back, locked eyes, and then coquettishly looked away.

In a moment, he approached.

"Excuse me, do I know you?" He looked ever-so-slightly embarrassed at his own transparency.

"I don't think so," she answered with a smile that invited further conversation.

"Yeah, I didn't think so," he went on. "I never know anybody I want to know. I know a lot of people I don't want to know and a few people who don't want to know me, but I hardly ever know the people I want to know. Know what I mean?"

There were two responses open to her. Another smile, which might be effective but required more coaxing on his part, or a laugh, which would put him totally at ease. She laughed.

"I'm Hal Fisher, and obviously I'm lousy at picking up beautiful women."

"No, you're very good at it, but I'm sorry. I don't want to be picked up."

Then the reassuring smile.

"Of course not. I'm sorry." And he looked as if he genuinely were. "But it's your own fault for looking like Lana Turner in *The Postman Always Rings Twice*."

Another laugh was necessary to prevent him from returning to his friends.

"That's the sweetest compliment I've ever received." The laugh became a gentle smile that demanded that he continue.

"Look," he said, avoiding her pale blue eyes, "see that guy over there?" He indicated one of his group.

"Yes."

"His name's Bernie Lochman and that's his wife Reenie and they're the nicest people in the world. If we were introduced by them, then it wouldn't be me trying to pick you up, it would be us meeting through

mutual friends, which is the nicest way to meet, so
why don't I ask them to introduce us?''

"But I don't know them." Audrey protested just
enough, no more.

"Then I'll introduce you." Hal had taken her by
the arm, and Audrey followed easily, wondering
whether she would actually like this man but knowing
the odds were that he was like all the others.

"Excuse me." This man's voice was different, and
it was more than a decade later.

Audrey looked up to see the *Esquire* magazine hawk
standing above her.

"May I buy you a drink?"

She had been dreading the trip to her mother's
house, dreading it even though it would be cut short
by news of a joyous tragedy. She had almost changed
her mind and canceled the ticket. But now she was
glad she hadn't.

"Yes." And she smiled the smile that was by now
honed to perfection.

18

Frieda Altshul sat across the breakfast table from her husband as she had done for twenty-eight years, staring at the back pages of the *Wall Street Journal*. From the other side of that formidable newspaper, a voice decreed, "Lamb for dinner would be nice."

"Yes, dear."

"And tell Bernie to be careful mowing around the cutting garden. Last time he ran over the foxgloves."

"I'll tell him."

A hand holding an empty coffee cup protruded from around the paper. Frieda immediately filled it with coffee, milk, and one and a half Sweet 'n Lo's. The hand disappeared, and the clink of spoon on china was heard.

"I don't suppose you picked up my tennis racket yet." The voice held a trace of exasperation.

"Not yet, dear."

"No, I didn't think so."

"I am driving into town today. I'll pick it up then."

"Good."

The hand reappeared, felt around for a stack of toast, found it, and disappeared with a slice.

She could see the top of Frank's head over the newspaper. His hair, which should have been gray, was brown, but the transformation was beautifully done. The stylist, for that was what barbers had decided to be called, used several shades to make it appear more natural.

She wondered if Frank's secretary, the one he was having the affair with, had put him up to it. She had the right; the affair had lasted fourteen years so far. That was twice the tenure of a common-law wife; but of course that didn't apply, since Frank had a legal wife already. The one who filled his cup with coffee the exact color and sweetness he liked and who went from market to market to find lamb when he wanted lamb and who fetched his tennis racket and instructed the once-a-week gardener and the once-a-week pool man and the twice-a-week cleaning woman. She even arranged the four-times-a-year visits from his son, who also was very particular about his coffee and his garden.

"Shall we have some of my men and their wives round for a barbecue on Saturday?"

"If you like."

"Call them, will you?"

"Of course. Who would you like to have?"

"The list is on the coffee table in the den."

How nice to be consulted about it, she thought, but there was no bitterness in it, merely amusement.

Shortly thereafter, Frieda heard Frank's cup placed in its saucer with a clink of finality. The *Wall Street Journal* was lowered, folded twice, and handed to her. Why, she'd never fathomed, since he knew perfectly well she didn't read it. But that was his custom, and Frank Altshul was a man to whom custom was as nourishing as bread was to others. She followed him to the entry hall, as she had done a lifetime of times before, handed him his briefcase, opened the door, presented her cheek, received her kiss, and closed the door.

Then she went swiftly upstairs to their bedroom and got the revolver she had hidden among her stockings.

It was certainly dreadful-looking, and the man had assured her it would leave a hole into which you could slip your fist. The bullets, however, were rather attractive. Like metallic penises, she mused as she put the box of them into her purse with the gun.

Hal Fisher's address and the address of Studio 104 were already on a neatly folded slip of paper in her change purse.

As she came downstairs, the twice-weekly cleaning woman was in the entry hall.

"Mattie," she said gently and respectfully, "Mr. Altshul asked if you would repolish his tennis trophies."

"Asked?" the elderly Irish woman said with a smirk.

"Would you like coffee? There's some on the stove. I'm going into the city." She took a jacket from the closet, tucked her purse under her arm, feeling the hardness of the gun, and left.

19

Hal and Betty sat on a bench in the police station, arm in arm, quietly watching the routine tragedies of the morning. A young black with a look of practiced hatred sat across from them, and when their eyes met, his stared through them as if they didn't exist or were in danger of ceasing to exist. A white woman whose purse had been ripped from her was describing the girl who'd done it to a policeman at a desk. A sad-looking Puerto Rican who had failed to impress the police with the potential violence of his landlord walked back and forth, afraid to leave. A stoned kid hung around the watercooler, laughing to himself.

"You're waiting to see Sergeant Winitsky?" A young man in street clothes approached them.

"Yeah."

"I'm sorry, but he's on vacation."

"What?!" Hal yelped, and the stoned kid smiled over at him. "We were here last night. Nobody said anything then about his being on vacation."

"I guess they didn't know." The young cop smiled, trying to apologize for some of the guys he knew were idiots. "He's off for the week."

"I can't wait a goddamn week. What kind of crap is this?"

"Sir, is there someone we can talk to?" Betty returned the cop's smile, hoping to make him an ally before Hal alienated him.

"You can talk to me."

He showed them into another small room like the small room in which Hal had faced Winitsky the Disbeliever.

And the same thing happened.

But this one, being less practiced at presenting only official reactions, almost laughed in Hal's face.

"You mean to tell me every one of these guys was murdered by his wife?" He glanced at the list Hal had given him, the list that began with Terrell and ended with Fisher.

"No, dammit, this is the *last* list! All these guys are alive. For Christ's sake, I'm the last one on it!"

"So where's the list of the dead guys?"

"I told you, Sergeant Winitsky has it."

"But he didn't do anything about it."

"That's right."

"Why not?"

"How should I know?! Maybe he didn't believe me. But now I can prove it!"

"How? With a list of men who are alive and kicking?"

"Listen to me! Try to listen to me, for Christ's sake—" Betty's hand clasped his, and he forced himself to suspend his hostility. "When I gave Sergeant Winitsky the first list, the last name on it was Federstein. And he was the only one who was still

155

alive. Now he's dead. I went to his wake yesterday. He's dead, like every other guy on that list. All anybody has to do is check on when I gave the list to Winitsky and when Federstein died. How could I know beforehand he was going to die unless the list is what I say it is? And so is this one! It's the same fucking list, with one slight difference. My name's on it! And I don't intend to sit around and let the fucking police laugh at me until I'm dead!''

The policeman nodded slowly, and it was unclear whether he was nodding in sympathy, understanding, or belligerence.

"Winitsky will be calling in. I'll tell him you were here."

"That's all you intend to do?!"

"If he has the list you gave him, we'll do some checking. Leave this list with me. I'll call the men on it. What else can I do?"

After Hal and Betty were gone, the policeman did indeed make a phone call. He reached Malcolm Terrell, who told him that Hal Fisher was a lunatic with an obsession and ought to be locked up. The policeman agreed, and tacked the list up on his bulletin board, more as a curiosity than anything else.

20

Johanna Davis, dressed to kill, sat in Hal's outer office waiting for him. On the couch next to her were two old sitcom scripts she had stolen from her husband Paul's study. He'd written them years before when he'd attempted to become a writer; they were not good, but it didn't matter. She had retyped the title page with the pseudonym Jane Sommerhill, half for her roommate in college with whom she had fallen in love and half, as a touch of whimsy, for the dorm monitor who'd reported them.

On top of the old scripts (she hoped Fisher wouldn't notice they were slightly yellowed with age) sat her purse, and inside that a bottle of pills that lowered blood pressure to such an extent that, combined with alcohol, they caused cardiac arrest. It was her intention to seduce Hal Fisher of 166 Central Park West while applying for a job writing for his show, to go to a hotel with him, and to ply him with champagne and as many pills as she could get into him. It was then her plan to fly to the Pritikin Institute in California and stay there until someone called to tell her Paul was dead.

She had already bought the dark blue suit for his funeral, at Loehmann's, for half the price at Oscar de la Renta.

"If you want coffee, help yourself," Andy said as he came out of his office and headed for the door. "I've got to get down to the studio and explain to the director who Diane Arbus is so he can explain it to Glenda so she can pronounce it wrong tonight so the audience won't get the joke. You sure you want to write this stuff?"

"Very sure."

"Okay, good luck. Hal ought to be in any minute. Or not. These days nobody knows."

Alone, Johanna wondered why the young man hadn't given her the appreciative look she was used to. Today of all days, with her dressed to kill.

Literally.

A half hour later, Betty entered the writers' office and found Johanna Davis polishing her toenails.

"Sorry," the latter said, flushed with embarrassment, "but nobody's here and I've been waiting so long . . ." She removed her feet from the coffee table and hid them beneath it.

"Can I help you?"

"I have an appointment with Mr. Fisher. I'm Jane Sommerhill."

"An appointment? For today?"

"That's right."

"He didn't say anything . . ."

"Well, it was arranged by a mutual friend. Vincent

158

Harding. I brought some of my scripts.'' She indicated the short stack beneath the purse and pills.

"I'm sorry, but he's not coming in today.''

"He isn't? But that's terrible! I mean, I'm only going to be in New York today. I really have to see him. Do you have any idea where he is?''

"I know exactly where he is. Where I sent him.''

Hal sat in a theater two blocks from Studio 104 watching a horror movie. Betty was right. Sitting there in the damp darkness, smelling the aroma of popcorn and watching his favorite silly art form, he felt weightless for a while.

He was safe, he reminded himself. He was last on the list. He had time. Time for Winitsky to come back and finally take him seriously. Time to beat the truth out of Audrey if necessary.

Audrey.

Where was she? He had called the apartment four times between waking up and taking this cool leather seat, and still no answer. Good. What would he say to her? Better for Winitsky to be the one to tell her.

And whatever they did to her, that was all right with him. He wouldn't interfere. He wouldn't beg for clemency. If she went to prison, he wouldn't visit her or look back. He would get on with the rest of his life.

Sitting there in the dark, he'd never felt so homeless, so lost, or so dissociated in his life.

*   *   *

Betty opened one of Jane Sommerhill's scripts out of curiosity. The woman had left angrily when Betty refused to tell her where Hal was. She hoped the scripts were rotten, for she didn't like the idea of Hal working with a woman who was so much prettier than she. If there was any fairness in the world, all good writers would look like Dame Edith Sitwell or Lillian Hellman.

Luckily, the script was execrable.

21

Jane Klemm's secretary and her cook were squabbling over who'd told her laundress to add starch to the wash water and the corgis were yelping and the phone was ringing and the answering machine was announcing that she was still in the Hamptons and the wallpaper hanger was dribbling paste on the parquet and she thought she would go mad.

She announced to all her intention of soaking in a hot tub and that she was in for no one and would answer no questions and in the words of Greta Garbo *wanted to be alone!*

Even the dogs were excommunicated.

She settled back in the hot, bubbly water and thought about all the things she had to think about.

Her prenuptial agreement. She had to talk to her lawyer about it or convince Todd to rescind it, for as his widow she would feel no loyalty to his foundation.

The florist. No pink roses. Absolutely no pink roses.

Call her masseuse and beg off for the next few days. Too much to do.

Remind her lover to get tickets to *Phantom* for her secretary.

Put the Sabatier knife with the seven-inch blade into her alligator purse, the one that opened easily, so she could get it out quickly and dispose of Mr. . . . what was his name? Fisher. Hal Fisher.

Call Todd's secretary and remind her to remind Todd that Friday was their anniversary and Mr. Melton at Cartier knew what she wanted.

Send the dogs to the groomers.

22

There was a sign in front of Studio 104 that read: *Family Business. Taped Before a Live Audience. Today at 4.* Two network pages were handing out free tickets, and various passersby were snapping them up.

Including Frieda Altshul.

"Excuse me, young man," she said, twinkling at one of the pages to give her lie the innocence of truth, "I'm Mr. Fisher's aunt. Do you know if he'll be at the taping?"

"I'm sorry, I don't know who Mr. Fisher is," the boy replied.

"Mr. Hal Fisher? He writes the show."

"Oh, sure, him. Yeah, he'll be here."

"Thank you." Frieda glanced at her watch. It was shortly after one, which was perfect; she had time to visit the little needlepoint shop on Second Avenue and see what new designs they had.

Johanna Davis, a.k.a. Jane Sommerhill, arrived downstairs from Hal's office after the pages had gone back to the network building. She paused in the lobby.

"Can I help you?" a guard behind a desk inquired.

"I had an appointment with Hal Fisher, but he seems to have forgotten."

"Well, he should be here for this afternoon's taping, if you want to come back," the guard said sympathetically.

"Really? That would be perfect. Thank you." She turned to leave, and stopped abruptly. "Only I don't have a ticket. Could you give me one?"

"No problem." The guard opened the top drawer of the desk and withdrew a stack of rubber-banded passes. He slid one out with difficulty and handed it to her.

"Thanks a lot." She turned, and hesitated. "Is there a housewares store around here?"

"There's one around the corner on Seventh."

"Thanks again."

She went off to buy a knife, and halfway down the block Johanna passed a trash can and deposited the bottle of blood-pressure pills in it. She had been looking forward to making love with a big-time TV writer, but what the hell, killing one was just as good.

A limousine pulled up outside Studio 104 a little after three and the driver, a black man in full chauffeur regalia, got out, entered the lobby, and walked smartly up to the guard.

"I'm here for the Klemm ticket."

The guard, also black, disliked brothers in uniforms of subservience, and he got out the VIP list more slowly than usual.

"Nobody by that name here. How do you spell it?"

"K-L-E-double-M." His tone was haughty.

"Nope. Nobody here." The guard smiled widely.

The driver pursed his lips and rose up as straight as he could, adding an inch or two to his height.

"Have you ever heard of Todd Klemm?"

He wanted to play hotshot? That was fine with the guard.

"Nope, but I love games. Have you ever heard of Leo Durocher?"

"Mr. Klemm is a *very important man*." He stressed each word separately.

"No kidding? Is your massah more important than my massah?"

"And Mrs. Klemm is waiting in the car," he said, glowering.

"And Mrs. Durocher was Laraine Day. I'm having a great time, how about you?"

The chauffeur, having exhausted every avenue of condescension he knew, left.

A moment later Betty and Andy entered the lobby from the studio on their way to the street.

"Are you sure you won't have lunch with us?" Betty asked.

"Not me. Two's company, three's a story conference. Besides, I'm on my way to Bloomingdale's. It's like no other store in the world."

Andy stopped by the desk. "Hey, Martin."

"Hi, Andy."

"How's the house today? Are we going to have an audience?"

"Not bad. Still got a lot of passes left, though."

"Well, get out there and force them on people." Andy pushed open the glass front door as Jane Klemm approached it. She went through ahead of him without a thank-you and walked straight to the guard.

"I'm Jane Klemm. Do you have a ticket for me?" she commanded.

Martin smiled. It was going to be a fun afternoon. "Was that your boy who came in before?"

"That was my chauffeur, but I neglected to give him the price of the ticket." She held out her hand, and there was a hundred-dollar bill in it.

Martin smiled again, more broadly this time, and ripped two tickets in half on the rubber band before getting one out whole for her.

23

"Do me a favor," Hal said. "Let me see you eat something with a couple of vitamins in it."

The waitress winked at him. She knew Betty and the junk she put in her body.

"I'll have a western omelet, side of string beans, and a large O.J.," Betty said, sulking.

"Bless your heart," the waitress said, taking her menu. "What about you?"

"The same but instead of the string beans I'll have french fries and instead of the orange juice I'll have a diet Coke."

"Sure, he can dish it out, but he can't take it," the waitress said, and left them in peace.

"How was your movie?"

"Gruesome and very funny. This woman's face melted off her and—"

"Spare me. I don't like horror movies."

"How can you not like horror movies? They fulfill a basic need."

"What need?"

"The need to face our worst fears and triumph over them."

"Did the woman without a face triumph?"

"No, the audience did. We all got out of the theater alive and well, except for the stains on our ties from the plastic butter on the popcorn."

"How can you watch that junk?"

"Hey, from now on you're going to have to go to a lot of horror movies, so watch your mouth."

Betty smiled secretly. "You know what I'd like?" she responded.

"What?"

"When this is all over, I'd like to rent a car and drive up to Cape Cod. I'd like to eat two lobsters in a row and buy something I can't afford from a country slicker in an antique shop and bring home dumb presents for Andy like ceramic seagulls and a lamp made out of shells . . ."

That's the way life's supposed to be, Hal thought, looking at Betty's childlike smile. But somehow it had never been like that with Audrey.

Not even on their honeymoon. They'd been in Saint Thomas in the tangle of shopping streets, two little fish in a frenzied school of tourists buying everything in sight. All except Audrey. She was right, of course. The clothes that seemed so charming there would be tacky in New York; the ornaments he found amusing and gay would go in the back of a closet in the coop Audrey had selected. No, they were to have a *lifestyle,* not a life.

"Penny for you thoughts." Betty pulled a shiny new cent from her changepurse and put it in his hand.

"I was just thinking I'd like a lamp made out of sea shells."

24

Sergeant Winitsky, in a sports jacket and T-shirt, entered the police station.

"Hey, Winitsky, I thought you were on vacation," someone tacking up announcements on a bulletin board called to him.

"I am. You never saw me."

He pushed through the door that led to the bullpen and saw his favorite local prostitute sitting at one of the desks, waiting to be questioned or verbally spanked. She was thirteen years old.

"Hiya, Carmen."

"Hello, Winitsky. Got a cigarette?"

"Come on, you'll stunt your growth," he said, and tossed her one anyway.

In his office, he was searching through his desk when Officer Brice came in, all smiles.

"What're you doing here? I thought you and Anne were going to Maine."

"We are, as soon as I find my goddamn card case."

"What kind of cards?"

"The kind that pay for a trip to Maine. You know, AmEx, MasterCard . . ."

"You lost them?"

"They're not at home. If they're not here, yeah, I lost them."

"Sorry."

"If you're so sorry, what're you smiling about?"

"This." She extended her hand, and Winitsky looked at the smallest diamond ring he'd ever seen. "Fred and I are doing it."

"No kidding."

"Uh-huh. We're the first interracial couple on the block."

"Not on this block, honey." He flipped through a pile of papers on his desk.

"Fred, come in here," Brice called out to the bullpen, and in a moment the young man who had so offended Hal entered the room. The two officers shook hands.

"I hear congratulations are in order."

"Either that or warnings."

"Or a little bit of both."

"Hey, you guys . . ." Brice smirked.

"May you be happier than Anne's going to be if I don't find my charge cards." He went back to searching.

"We'll help." Brice and her fiancé began rooting among his papers.

"Thanks, guys. So, when's the happy day?"

"Probably in two weeks," Brice answered.

"Or three," from Fred.

"You trying to get out of marrying me?"

"Would it do any good?"

"No way, Jose."

"Thank God!" Winitsky almost shouted, holding up a small leather card case, which he'd found at the back of his second drawer. "I love you both, have a great life, I'm on my way to Maine!" He hurried for the door.

"Wait a minute," Fred said, and his dark tone stopped Winitsky in his tracks. "What's this?"

He held up a piece of paper with the names of six dead men on it.

25

It was quarter to four, and the audience started to file in. There were the unemployed, the housewives, teenagers home from and cutting school, out-of-towners, children with their mothers and au pairs and sitters, the chronically ill who had been around the corner at the hospital, a group of retarded adults, a busload from Hackensack, New Jersey, the neighborhood regulars, network employees, hopeful actors, and Frieda Altshul.

She said, in a small and winning voice, to the page who took her ticket at the door, "Do you know if Mr. Hal Fisher is here? I'm his aunt."

"I haven't seen him, but the writers don't usually come down until after the warm-up. Shall I have someone call upstairs and tell him you're here?"

"No, thank you. I'd rather surprise him." And Frieda passed into the lobby with the crowd that was hurrying into the studio to get the best seats. She pressed her purse to her side and felt the reassuring hardness of the gun she had bought for only forty-nine dollars and ninety-five cents. Somehow, she'd always thought firearms were more expensive. And they certainly should be, she tsk-tsked to herself, to keep them out of the wrong hands.

She followed the crowd into the studio, and immediately felt a shock of recognition when there, not thirty feet from her, was the home of Glenda Carpenter laid out room by room on an enormous stage. But the rooms were disturbingly out of order: the office of *Family Business* stood between Glenda's bedroom, with its pretty blue and white wallpaper, and the family kitchen, whose cupboards were, in reality, not the color they appeared to be on her TV screen, and certainly not as new or clean. And as if that weren't enough to confound the audience, the family bathroom stood off to one side of the stage alone, and next to it, of all things, there was a jail cell! It was all too haphazard for poor Frieda. She felt quite dazed by it.

A page was indicating the proper tier of seats for her and those near her to occupy, and Frieda was carried with the crowd and deposited in one of them.

She would stay put until the warm-up (whatever that was) was over and then pardon herself, climb down from her row, and find Mr. Hal Fisher, whereupon she would put a hole into his head large enough for her to place her fist through (if the man who sold her the gun could be trusted) and then get the car and go home. Dinner for Frank was already made and he never got home before seven. All was very well organized indeed.

At that moment, in the outside lobby, Johanna Davis was inquiring after Hal.

26

Winitsky hung up the phone and looked at Fred solemnly.

"Federstein was killed in a boating accident a couple of days ago."

"You're kidding me."

"I'm not. And neither was Fisher." He picked up the phone again and glanced at Hal's number, scrawled at the bottom of the list.

"You mean you really think there's some kind of conspiracy?" Brice started to laugh.

"Hey, there's always a chance." Winitsky dialed. "And to tell you the truth, there's something about this that's too weird to be bullshit. I mean, a guy brings you a list, you think he's a kook. He brings you two lists, and the guy he says is dead *is* dead, and you begin to wonder."

The phone rang in Hal's apartment, but neither Hal in his haste nor Audrey in hers had taken the time to turn on the answering machine.

"Nobody's home. What did this guy say he did for a living?"

27

Hal and Betty were crossing the lobby to the writers' office for their weekly sugar high when a woman in the crowd, Jane Klemm, elbowed them out of her way.

"Take it easy, lady. It's not that good," Hal called after her. He opened the door to see Andy and Arthur separate quickly. Andy smiled devilishly at them; Arthur turned a bright vermilion.

"Hey, nobody gets kissed around here unless the boss gets kissed first." Hal presented his cheek to Andy and pointed to it. Andy beamed, kissed his check, and winked at Arthur, who pretended he had to check his equipment and left hastily.

"Is he ever going to relax?" Hal snatched a Mounds bar from the table.

"Who knows? Thanks for trying."

"So, what's on for today?"

"Well, in case you forgot," Betty started, "today Glenda gets a parking ticket, but will she pay the two dollars?"

"No way!" she and Andy intoned together.

"Our Glenda goes to court," Betty continued,

"where she is her own defense attorney, and when the judge sides with the traffic cop and tells her to pay, what does she say?"

"No way!" Andy joined in again.

" 'Even if you put me in jail, I will not pay!' " Betty orated. " 'This is a matter of principle!' "

"So they put her in jail," Andy said. "And does she pay?"

"Bet your ass." Betty sat down.

"What a piece of shit." Hal nodded sadly. "Whose idea was that?"

"Yours."

"I like it. Where's the sodas?"

"Missing."

"I'll get them." Hal crossed to the door. "Usual poison?"

"Anything with chemicals in it."

"And Arthur and I will have root-beer floats. He likes his with butter pecan ice cream," Andy said proudly.

"Two Diet Cokes, coming up." Hal left.

He crossed the lobby and entered the studio, where the warm-up man was finishing with the visitors from the tri-state area and had found gold in a family from Alaska.

". . . Alaska, ladies and gentlemen! Funny, you don't look Eskimo. Today's show is sad. I hope you don't blubber. And give it your seal of approval . . ."

Hal crossed the side of the stage, heading toward the prop room and its refrigerator full of sodas.

"Hold it! Ladies and gentlemen, you see that man skulking across our stage? That man is none other than Hal Fisher, the head writer of *Family Business*."

The audience applauded, and Hal glanced back at them over his shoulder and waved, uncomfortable as ever when faced with the crowd.

Frieda Altshul lowered her glasses to get a good look at him.

Johanna Davis stood up halfway.

Jane Klemm stared at him through mother-of-pearl opera glasses as he disappeared behind the living room back wall.

Frieda, Johanna, and Jane stood up in unison and started down the aisles. When the pages stopped them, one by one, from crossing the stage after Hal, they took three separate detours. Frieda asked where the ladies' room was. Johanna asked if there was a public phone. Jane said the anti-Alaskan remarks offended her and stormed out. One ended up downstairs searching the catacomb of hallways that led, properly traversed, to the backstage area and the prop room, where Hal was chatting with the assistant propman while balancing three Diet Cokes in his hands; another found an alley hallway that took her to the far side of the stage and the quick-change area; the third sneaked behind the jail set when no one was watching and was hurrying, unknowingly, toward the green room.

28

Winitsky clenched his teeth. The network secretary on the other end of his phone call was getting to him.

"Look, miss, this is Sergeant Edward Winitsky of the New York City Police Department and I want to talk to Hal Fisher *now*. I don't want any excuses or any reasons why I can't talk to him. I don't want to leave a message and I don't want to talk to your supervisor or your boss or Walter Cronkite. I want to talk to Hal Fisher!"

"Sir, I'm trying to tell you, Mr. Fisher doesn't work here. He's employed by Westbank Entertainment, but you won't reach him there either—"

"Miss, maybe you don't understand—"

"Please hold." The secretary clicked off, and Winitsky's teeth dug into his lips.

He had hoped to talk to Fisher briefly, assure himself that everything was all right for the moment, assign someone else to the case, and get the hell to Maine. But until he spoke to Fisher himself, that was impossible. It opened the department up to all kinds of accusations.

"Officer?" The secretary was back. "Mr. Fisher is at Studio 104 on Broadway right now. They're taping his show. Would you like the number there?"

"No, I better see him in person," he said, changing his plan. "Just the address."

29

Hal left the prop room, three sweating cans of Diet Coke in his hands, passed the stage entrance, went down the hall to the stairs that led beneath the stage to the hall that split in two. He took the right-hand path, past the men's room, the green room, the engineers' room, the pay phone, and the ladies' room, to the staircase that led up to the lobby, the control and sound booths, and, finally, the writers' office.

At precisely the same time, Frieda Altshul was meticulously filling her gun with bullets in the ladies' room. The task completed, she peeked out into the hall, saw that no one was there, and hurried away in the direction from which Hal had come.

Johanna Davis hurried down the hallway that led to the stairs that led to the stage entrance and prop room. Johanna was hopelessly lost, having been past the actors' dressing rooms, the wardrobe department, makeup, and the extras' green room. She clutched her knife behind her back and hurried past the men's room, green room, engineers' room, and ladies' room to the staircase that Hal had taken, in time to pass Jane Klemm, who was scurrying downstairs.

"Do you know where—" Jane started.

"No!" Johanna snapped, taking the stairs two at a time.

"Bitch." Jane felt in her purse for the knife and turned left past the green room.

Meanwhile, Hal, in the safety of the writers' office, was pontificating to his cohorts on sitcoms as the twentieth-century art form most directly descended from Restoration comedy.

30

Winitsky, still in sports jacket and T-shirt, was driving north on Eighth Avenue. He had both lists in his pocket; the first, of six dead men whose deaths might or might not be attributed to foul play; the second, of six men who might or might not be in danger. He had photocopied the second list before leaving the station and put Fred in charge of a team that was contacting each man and asking him to come to Winitsky's office the following day, where, if Fisher proved to be telling the truth, they would be met and possibly put into protective custody by Andrew Dowaliby, Winitsky's fiercest competitor on the force and the only man he trusted with this case.

If, indeed, it was a case. If, in truth, Fisher was not a total lunatic.

He had briefly toyed with the idea of putting off his vacation until this bizarre thing was settled one way or the other, but then, remembering that Anne had seen a marriage counselor three times and a divorce lawyer once, he decided not to.

He was thinking of the lawyer and not his driving

when he turned the car east just as a van was pulling out of an illegal parking spot.

Winitsky's car sideswiped the back of the van just hard enough to send his head crashing into the side window of his car, and that hard enough for him to lose consciousness.

31

Frieda came upon the stage entrance, and the door-man, who was losing his daily battle with the crossword puzzle, looked up from a six-letter word meaning "rift" and saw her.

"Can I help you?"

"I'm looking for Mr. Hal Fisher."

"Mr. Fisher's out front."

"But I just saw him come backstage."

"Yeah, and then he went down those stairs to the front of the house."

"Oh. Thank you very much."

Frieda turned to pursue her quarry, and that was when she dropped her gun. She and the doorman stared at it, lying on the ground.

"Oh, dear," Frieda said, snatching it up and pointing it at the man. "Would you mind coming with me?"

"Okay, lady, just don't use that thing. I got four kids."

"Four children? On a doorman's salary? Good heavens." She hurriedly looked around and saw a doorway. "What's in there?"

"Just a room."

"What's it used for?"

"Nothing. It's empty."

"Excellent. Would you go in there?" She brandished the revolver and the doorman stepped lively.

Once inside, Frieda looked around for something with which to tie him up. There was nothing. Nor was there a lock on the door.

Having no alternative, she held the gun to the frightened man's temple. He closed his eyes and whispered, "Please," as she turned the revolver in her hand and brought the butt down on his head as hard as she could.

What followed was exactly the same as portrayed in the movies.

The man crumpled to the floor and lay there motionless. With enormous difficulty, Frieda pushed the limp body into a cupboard, which happily had a combination lock hanging from two clasps in front. She closed the doors and spun the lock. Then, when her heart pounded more softly in her breast, she left the room, closing the door after her.

32

As luck would have it, Winitsky was merely unconscious and was taken to the emergency room of a hospital directly around the corner from Studio 104.

When he started to wake, lying on a stretcher in a hallway, he was at first unfocused and disoriented. He had the vague feeling that he and his wife were in a rowboat on a lake in Maine, but they were fogbound. Slowly the fog lifted, and a marriage counselor, a young woman dressed in white, was leaning in, saying something to him.

"I don't understand," he replied to her words, which blended together.

"Please lie still," she repeated, and he thought she wasn't a marriage counselor at all but a hooker from the station.

And then, briefly, she was his wife, and finally, a nurse.

"Where am I?" His head pounded as he spoke.

"You're in the hospital. You'll be fine."

But he didn't feel fine. The fog was coming in again, and her words, meant to soothe and comfort him, were drifting off across the water.

33

Jane Klemm hurried up a flight of stairs and found herself in one corner of the vast soundstage, behind the sets. She could hear the actors saying their lines over a loudspeaker and near her as well.

"Mom, I'm not a kid."

"And you're not grown up, either. I know. I'm still paying for your underwear."

She stepped forward and saw a gaudily made-up young woman sitting at a makeup table against the wall. A man with a comb in one hand and a spray can in the other fussed with her hair.

"I'll talk to Dad."

"Fine. He could use a good laugh."

She knew she mustn't be seen, and stepped back into the shadows by the stairwell. But there were voices, hushed women's voices. She looked down the stairs and there, coming up, were half a dozen extras, all of whom would see her and be able to identify her should the worst happen.

Where to hide?

"When I have kids . . ."

"I'll be on their side. There's no justice in a family."

Forward, the woman and the hairdresser. Backward, and the extras (dressed as prostitutes and heading no doubt for the jail) would be all around her.

"No wonder kids run away from home."

"The big suitcase is in the back of my closet."

She looked around frantically. There, behind her, was the back of a wall of some sort with a door in it. It was covered with spray-painted letters and numbers. If she put her face down and hurried, she could be through that door before anyone got a decent look at her.

She rushed through.

The first sign that she had made a dreadful mistake was the blinding white light that forced her eyes closed momentarily. When she opened them, Glenda Carpenter and her television son were staring at her in stunned silence, along with three hundred audience members.

She was standing in their kitchen.

"Who the hell is that?" Stu's voice boomed out over a loudspeaker.

"Anybody send out for pizza?" Glenda asked, and there was laughter and applause.

Jane turned to flee through the same doorway through which she'd entered, but it was filled with prostitutes laughing at her.

She covered her face with her purse and ran through the kitchen to the darkness of the unlit sets and the far wall of the studio. There she found a real doorway, pushed through it, and sighed with relief to find herself in an alley.

She had been seen. *Seen?* She had guest-starred on a TV show. And probably been taped into the bargain!

She started out of the alley toward the street, cursing as she did. Now she had no choice but to go home and hope that one of the others would dispose of Hal Fisher.

She was livid with disappointment.

34

Hal entered the control room, fought his way through a cluster of laughing producers, and bent over Stu's shoulder.

"How many times I gotta tell you to keep your mother off my show?"

"Who *was* that?" Stu spoke into the mike. "Sorry, madam, the bathroom is downstairs."

"She doesn't need it anymore," Glenda quipped, and the audience went wild.

"All right, let's start with Kevin's entrance," Stu continued over the laughter. "People, please. You want to laugh? Wait till we're taping, and you'll hear yourself laugh at home. . . ."

Hal turned to the producers. "Anybody got a cigarette?"

"Hey, what're you doing?" an assistant-associate-coordinating producer asked. "You quit last season."

"Yeah, but I'm still owed one."

Three producers held out packs to him.

THE LAST MAN ON THE LIST

"Eeny, meeny, miney . . ." Moe was a Marlboro Light, his old beloved brand. He lit up and left the control room, traversed the sound booth, where two of the guys were in the midst of what appeared to be a four-year gin rummy game, and entered the lobby.

Where Johanna Davis was standing.

35

Sergeant Winitsky finally awoke completely to find not one, but two nurses standing by his stretcher, paying no attention to him but engrossed in their own conversation.

". . . I already put in a double shift and I don't give a damn what McMillan says. Eight o'clock and I'm out of here." The speaker, the elder of the two, was clearly in mid-tirade.

"I don't blame you. How can you do your best when you're exhausted?" The younger, eager-to-please one clucked her support.

"I'm only a human being, not a machine."

"Exactly."

He started to speak, found no sound coming forth, and cleared his throat.

"You're awake." The older one turned and told him what he already knew. "Just lie there. One of the doctors will be with you in a minute."

"Where am I?" Sound came.

"You're in the hospital." The older nurse's tone was cold and strict, and Winitsky knew they wouldn't get along.

"No shit. Which hospital?"

"Just lie still. The doctor will—"

"Which hospital?!"

"St. Teresa's." She spat out the words, affronted.

Winitsky rose on one elbow and with his free hand reached for his wallet and badge.

"Just a minute, sir," the elder nurse said, and the younger one stared in disbelief at the man who dared to disregard her superior's command. "You'll have to lie down until the doctor gets here. You've been in an accident."

He had difficulty extricating his wallet from his pants pocket, and that annoyed him as much as the condescension of the nurse. "I know I was in an accident. You don't have to tell me."

"Then you should know you have to lie still."

"Please lie still," the other one parroted.

"Where are we?"

"You see?" The elder smirked smugly. "I already told you. In the hospital."

"I mean, where the hell is St. Teresa's?" He yanked the wallet free of the folds of his trousers and flipped it open to display his badge. The younger one blanched; the elder took it as a gauntlet thrown down, authority against authority.

"Fifty-fifth Street and Eighth Avenue, but you'll have to lie down . . ."

Winitsky sat up and tried not to listen to the scolding he was receiving. His head pounded, but not as badly as he'd expected.

". . . Sir, you have to lie down . . ."

One block to Broadway and the television studio where Hal Fisher worked.

". . . I cannot be responsible . . ."

He slid off the stretcher, and his knees buckled slightly as his feet hit the floor.

"Sir!"

He steadied himself on the edge of the stretcher. He'd felt worse than this. Lots of times.

"Will you please *obey* me?!" The elder nurse, livid with rage, was face to face with him now.

"Piss off, sweetheart," Winitsky said, heading down the hall.

Behind him he could hear the tirade continuing, much to his satisfaction.

36

". . . I will not pay the parking ticket!" Glenda's amplified voice rang out across the lobby, followed by a hearty round of applause.

Hal needed to make a pit stop before going back to the writers' office. He started for the stairs that led to the labyrinth of underground passageways.

He was thinking of whether or not to take up smoking again. He recalled with bittersweet fondness reaching for a cigarette while watching TV, the delicious action of lighting up and inhaling, the cozy busy-ness of puffing and flicking ashes and grinding out the depleted butt in an ashtray. And the downside: the filth of it, the coughing and phlegm and possible cancer and emphysema and heart attack, and the little offenses, the stench of his office and home and clothes and the looks people gave him when he lit up.

He entered the men's room and tossed the half-finished cigarette into the next urinal. No, he would not take up the habit again. If Audrey and her bevy of bitches didn't kill him, he certainly wouldn't do it for them.

It was the first time that day he'd thought of the danger he was in, being on that list.

And a prophetic time.

37

Winitsky hurried down the street between Eighth and Broadway and wished to God he had never become a cop. He was now a little dizzy, slightly nauseated, and quite sure that he had a mild concussion. It was his third; the first had been from a blow on the head at the hands of a teenage drug pusher, the second from diving off a diving boulder into a rich friend's pool. In both those cases, it had been his own damn fault.

He had once wanted to be a gym teacher. It sounded awfully good to him now.

Wouldn't it be funny, he mused, if he passed out and ended up on that stretcher again face to face with Nurse Ratchett?

Not funny at all, he decided.

38

The door behind him opened, but Hal stared ahead into his urinal. It was an unwritten law of men's rooms that one kept one's eyes where they belonged, directly ahead, for a sideways glance might be misconstrued.

There were footsteps on the hard bathroom tiles, unlike any footsteps he had ever heard in such a place.

They sounded like high heels.

Zipping up his fly, Hal turned.

Johanna Davis was standing not four feet from him; her hand with a carving knife in it was held high, aimed at him. She was frozen in an instant's catching of breath and screwing up of courage.

And then she lunged.

And Hal leaped to one side.

The knife hit the hard tile wall and the blade snapped in two. The lethal end clattered to the floor, but she lifted what was left of the blade and threatened Hal with that. He backed up.

"Jesus Christ!" His voice came out as little more than a whisper. "What're you doing?!"

She was opening her purse with her free hand.

"Oh, my God, you're one of them!" He understood now and continued to back toward the door, which was closer to him.

Johanna removed a second, identical carving knife from her purse and threw the broken one aside; it landed in Hal's unflushed urinal.

"Lady . . ." he pleaded. "Lady . . . for God's sake—"

She ran at him, her hand and the knife held high, her face twisted with a mixture of fear and almost sexual excitation. He grabbed the lethal wrist and held tight; they stood motionless for an instant, face to twisted face, hands quivering in isometric tension.

And then, with his free hand he pushed against her chest, and she lurched backward. In that instant, releasing her hand, Hal fled from the room.

Slamming the men's room door after him, he turned left and raced along the dimly lit passage to the stairs that led up to the stage entrance and the crowd that would absorb him.

". . . Your Honor, as counsel for my own defense, I ask for a continuum." Glenda's voice filled the narrow hallway and almost drowned out the clatter of high heels somewhere behind him. He grabbed the handrail and spun himself around to the bottom stair, and then, looking up toward safety, he saw a second woman at the top of the stairs.

"What does that mean, Mrs. McDowell?" the judge's voice boomed out in feigned irritation.

Hal spun into a second hallway downstairs and frantically looked for somewhere to hide.

"It means I can go home and make dinner," Glenda answered, and the audience laughed.

Johanna Davis did not see which way Hal went. She stopped at the foot of the stairs and looked up. There was no one there but a woman she didn't recognize, a friend of Glenda's who was late for the taping. Johanna instinctively chose the corridor into which Hal had fled.

39

Sergeant Winitsky entered the lobby of Studio 104, and a pretty young page standing in the corner reading a copy of the *National Enquirer* asked for his ticket. Her face became grave when she saw his badge and she solemnly escorted him to the writers' office.

It was there, with a confused Andy and a relieved Betty, that he sat down with a sigh of tiredness to wait for Hal's return.

40

Hal was hiding in a closet behind a rack of costumes, the reality of his terror quickly becoming fictionalized so he could bear it. It was all a movie-of-the-week he was writing. A well-earned change of pace from sitcomery. His friends would be surprised. *We didn't know you had it in you. A murder chain letter? Great idea, pal. And the bit with the lady writer? Smart. Nobody can accuse you of misogyny. Stop the VCR for a minute. I gotta pee.*

But there was no stopping this. There had been no stopping it for Woodward or Goodman or Federstein . . .

He heard muffled dialogue from above.

". . . I ask that that be stricken from the record and the jury advised to disregard it." Glenda got the line right for the first time.

"Mrs. McDowell, do you see a jury here?"

"No, Your Honor."

"That's right. This is a traffic violation, not a murder case."

That's what you think.

Suddenly there was light and the shrill whine of

metal sliding along metal as the costumes were thrust aside.

Johanna Davis stood there, knife on high, smiling at him.

"Hello," she whispered.

There was no way to stab at him overhand, for the closet rod was in the way; she attempted to jab at him chest-high, but that made it easy for Hal to grab her arm and pull with all his might. As she fell forward into the closet, Hal used her weight to pull himself out.

"You fuck!" she screamed, outraged, as he slammed the closet door and pressed his body against it.

"Your Honor, can I pay the fifteen dollars for my wife?" the husband's voice came down, and the audience applauded, drowning out Hal's call for help.

41

They had taken the policeman downstairs to the men's room to wash his perspiration-soaked face with cold water. Betty stood in the hallway outside, waiting for them, as Frieda Altshul descended the lobby stairs and approached her.

"Excuse me, do you know Mr. Hal Fisher?" she cooed.

"Yes." Betty smiled at the little pigeon of a woman.

"I'm looking for him. I'm his aunt."

"Really? I work for him."

"Then perhaps we can join forces and find him." Frieda pressed the purse under her arm to her side.

"He's probably backstage." Betty opened the men's room door a crack and called, "Guys, I'm going to go find Hal. We'll meet you upstairs in the office, okay?"

"Okay," Andy called back, distracted, for Winitsky was starting to retch.

42

". . . And my advice to you is to take her home and not allow her to watch *Perry Mason* reruns," the judge read his final line. A double take from Glenda and the scene would be over. From inside the closet, Hal could hear the woman's stream of filth as she slammed against the door.

"Help me!" he shouted, and upstairs the applause signs lit up and the audience once again drowned him out.

The extras would be coming down any second, now that the courtroom scene was over. He had only to keep his weight jammed against the door to be safe. Anything else was unthinkable. I am no hero, he thought. I am a fat comedy writer who married the wrong woman, but I am no hero.

Upstairs, the warm-up man, having time to kill during the costume change, opted to introduce the prostitutes to the audience one by one, thereby delaying Hal's rescue.

Again the woman slammed against the door, and succeeded in opening it a crack before Hal pressed it closed.

"Bastard!" the voice behind the door growled.

And then another voice, Betty's, called from down the hallway, "Hal?"

"Thank God!" he said, turning to see her coming toward him with a pleasant-looking older woman who was smiling sweetly at him and undoing the clasp of her purse.

"Get the police. I've got one of them in the closet."

"What?"

"One of the chain-letter women! She's trying to kill me!"

And from within the closet, a fresh stream of invectives.

"My God!" Betty gasped. "There's a policeman here!"

She turned in the direction of the men's room as Frieda Altshul removed the shiny, brand-new revolver from her purse and pointed it at her.

"Please don't," Frieda said simply. "Mr. Fisher, would you step aside?"

Fright had immobilized him, and she had to request it a second time before Hal went to Betty and the closet door opened. Johanna Davis stepped out of the closet triumphantly.

"I didn't know you were here," she said to Frieda.

"Yes, of course. Frank is before Paul on the list."

It occurred to Hal that he was right about the list, but any gratification that might have brought was overshadowed by the knowledge that unless he did something, something totally out of character for him, he would be the next to disappear from it. All he could do, however, was to plead Betty's case.

"Listen to me." His voice quavered. "She didn't have anything to do with this. Let her go, please!"

"How can we do that?" Frieda replied and, glancing at Johanna, she added, "It isn't possible, is it?"

"Of course not," Johanna snapped, smoothing her hair, which was still unkempt from her ordeal.

"Then we have no choice," Frieda said with more than a hint of regret.

"Look, you're not maniacs," Hal pleaded. "I don't know what your husbands are like or why they drove you to this, but this girl is innocent! She didn't do anything to anybody! For pity's sake . . ."

"You should have thought of that before you involved her, Mr. Fisher," Frieda said in her polite, logical way, and Hal knew she was right. He looked into Betty's fear-filled eyes and pleaded silently for her forgiveness. She gave it with a weak smile.

"Get in the closet," Johanna commanded. "Frieda, use that thing before it gets any later and the whole cast joins us down here."

"Oh, dear, yes, I'd hate to have to shoot Glenda Carpenter. I'm a fan of hers." She indicated the closet with the end of her gun. "Get in quickly."

"Jesus . . . please! . . ." Hal's voice whined uncontrollably.

"Get in!" This from Johanna.

"Please!"

"Mr. Fisher, into the closet. *Now!*" And for the first time, Frieda Altshul's voice filled with appropriate authority and became harsh.

He wanted to do something, but he couldn't. Shame mingled with fear and regret for Betty.

They turned, Hal and Betty, and stepped toward the closet.

Could they lock themselves in? His mind ricocheted from one desperate thought to another. *Would the door withstand bullets? Once inside, could he force Betty to the floor and shield her with his own body?*

"Get in," Frieda said, and now her voice was black with power.

They did as they were told.

If he attacked them, first reaching for the gun, accepting the burning slash of the other one's knife, would Betty have a chance to run? If he hurled himself against—

His thought was broken off by the thunderous sound of a gun going off.

He felt nothing, and Betty, beside him, holding his hand tightly, was also unaffected.

"Drop your gun and the knife."

It was a man's voice, a weary voice, but not pale with fear like his own. Hal turned and saw Sergeant Winitsky and Andy standing there.

From upstairs, a roar of laughter and applause.

"What the hell was that for?" Hal asked.

"I put the cannonball joke back in," Betty said, caving into his chest.

43

Hal and Betty sat in her tiny kitchen at the little table wedged against the wall. It was later that night, and in front of them, precariously balanced on the tabletop, were too many take-out cartons of Chinese food.

"Starting tomorrow," Hal said, reaching for his third fried dumpling, "we eat real food."

"What's unreal about this?"

"The secret of life is broccoli. And steamed carrots. And bran."

"Yes, Ma." She speared a hot and spicy shrimp.

Up to this point, Hal had said nothing about the shame he felt over his cowardice. But in his mind he saw himself walking to the costume closet over and over again, doing as he was told, accepting his death and Betty's for lack of courage, of manliness, of strength.

He could at least be man enough to own up to it.

"I'm sorry," he started.

"About what?"

"You know." Even now he would chicken out.

"I don't."

"That I didn't do anything. That I nearly let us get killed."

She smiled such a sweet smile at him that Hal was forced to smile back.

"I'm not much of a man," he said.

"Are you aware of what bullshit that is?" Betty wiped some grease from her lips with a dish towel from beside her on the sink.

"It's not bullshit. You missed a spot."

"Where?"

He took the towel from her and patted her chin.

"You really mean it?" Betty asked.

"Of course."

"You think you failed because you didn't get yourself killed?"

"I would've been killed either way. At least I could have done something about it." Normally, when he confessed to something, its power over him eased. This time, it worsened.

"What do they do to little boys to make them grow up into lunatics?" Betty took his hand. "You're not James Bond. You may not have noticed, but I'm not Emma Peel, either. I didn't do anything."

"You're not supposed to."

"Because I'm a woman? You want a load of feminist shit now or later?"

"That's not the point—"

"That's exactly the point. We're people. Normal, regular people. When somebody points a gun at us and says, 'Dance,' we turn into Fred Astaire and Ginger Rogers, just like everybody else except the demented idiots who think they're immortal. What're you apologizing for? For being sane?"

He hoped what she said would make a difference. In a few moments, he realized it didn't.

"I love you," Betty said finally, when the silence had lasted too long. "I never liked James Bond. He talks funny."

"Is that how you're going to deal with everything that comes up? By making a joke of it?"

"You know a better way?"

"One," he answered, overwhelmed by a feeling of tenderness for her. "Let's get out the bed."

"You talked me into it."

Betty opened the cupboard doors that hid the murphy bed and Hal pushed down on the mattress too hard, for the metal feet slammed on the floor.

"Sorry, Mr. Wong." Betty looked at the floor. "He's going to get me evicted one of these days."

Hal lay on the bed and held his arms open for Betty, who went into them with a sad delight, as if every wish she had ever had in her thirty-four years was being granted. She looked into his eyes with such concentration that Hal thought she was searching for his soul.

"I love you so much I want to cry," she said, and Hal wondered if he loved her as much. He wondered, and hoped that he did.

They kissed once before there was an angry knock at the door.

"Shit," Betty said, disengaging herself. "It's Mr. Wong come to complain."

She crossed to the door and opened it, prepared to spew forth apology after apology. Hal watched her, amused.

And then he saw Betty step backward into the room and Audrey come in after her.

With one hand Audrey closed the door; her other hand was tightly wrapped around a gun she had gotten from Joan, the priestess of murder.

"Get over there." She waved Betty to Hal's side. Her face was set, grim, and hate-filled.

"What're you doing here?!" Hal's voice once again rose to a whine.

"I didn't go to my mother's," she answered. "I got laid instead. But I've still got the ticket so I can prove I went. I'll go later, after you're dead."

Hal and Betty were standing by the bed, his arm around her, pulling her close, to no particular safety. Audrey stood by the door aiming the gun at them.

"Why?!" was all that Hal could say.

"Because I hate you," she answered. "And I can't live with you anymore and you owe it to me to die. . . ."

As her rage spewed out of her, Audrey's face took on a glow of relief, of triumph, of ultimate happiness.

". . . All these years of putting up with your crap and your self-importance. . . ."

And Hal found his own hatred starting to bubble within him, like a volcanic lake of acid. The loveless years, the years of pleading for affection and settling for a silent truce, came back to him. The times she'd hidden from him behind a book she had no interest in, the blame he'd shouldered for her unwillingness to join in, to be cheered or cheering. . . .

". . . Do you have any idea of what it's like to live with you?! With an unrelenting master of ceremonies?! . . ."

It wasn't true! he thought. If he was on all the time,

it was to cover her sullen shyness, the dour aloofness that hid her true fury at him and the world!

And offense after offense vomited out of his mind. Her dislike of his friends, whose wit she called "precious"; her accusations that he could never be intimate with anyone; her constant demeaning *lies;* the years that he had wasted on her, dismissing her coldness as his own neurotic need for love; the miserable lie that he had a bottomless pit no one could fill; the betrayals; the money thrown away; the affection withheld; the lies and lies and lies!

And without knowing it, Hal pushed Betty down to the safety of the bed and rushed toward his nemesis.

His hand went around hers like a steel glove, and she was unable to pull the trigger; his free arm was twisted around her throat. If he could have ripped her filthy head off, he would have.

Instead, they danced round and round, pushing against each other, their true mutual hatred joyously set forth, and still the memories came: the hurriedly ened phone calls when he walked into the room . . . the letter she'd written to a lover on the plane as they flew to Mexico, in which she said, "I wish you were here instead of him" . . . his own stupid self-loathing that had led him to marry her in the first place . . . his mother who'd overwhelmed him . . . his father who'd turned him into a competitor . . .

And, clenching his fist against all of them, Hal did what he had never done in his life.

He punched Audrey's face with all the rage of a thousand humiliations and disappointments.

She fell backward onto the murphy bed, unconscious.

"Quick!" Betty grabbed at the gun and, getting it, started to lift the bed.

They slammed it against the wall with Audrey in it and closed the doors over her.

And Hal, filled with an exhilaration he had never known, started to cry.

Betty went to the phone and dialed 911, and as she spoke to the police Hal looked at her and all doubt went away: he loved her as much as it was possible to love without decades of flowing together.

When she hung up the phone and came to him, he said simply, "Will you marry me?"